Adeline stood transfixed, frozen in fear, as the sports car barreled toward her.

Her brain screamed, *Move, now!* But her legs forgot how. A muscular arm snaked around her waist and jerked her backward. Lincoln pulled her close and dived into the yard.

"Are you okay?" he asked breathlessly.

The pounding of her heart in her throat made it impossible to form words, so she bobbed her head instead.

The sports car reversed then stopped even with their hiding place.

What was the guy waiting for? He had them trapped. If he had a weapon, why not open fire? Was he enjoying his little game of cat and mouse?

A silver king-cab truck turned onto the street. She immediately recognized it as belonging to her other boss, Ryan Vincent.

The sports car raced down the street.

Ryan pulled up beside where they stood on the sidewalk. The passenger side window rolled down. "What's going on?"

"They tried to run us down." Lincoln jerked open the passenger door, hopped in, slammed the door and yelled, "Follow them!"

Rhonda Starnes is a retired middle school language arts teacher who dreamed of being a published author from the time she was in seventh grade and wrote her first short story. She lives in North Alabama with her husband, whom she lovingly refers to as Mountain Man. They enjoy traveling and spending time with their children and grandchildren. Rhonda writes heart-and-soul suspense with rugged heroes and feisty heroines.

Books by Rhonda Starnes

Love Inspired Suspense

Rocky Mountain Revenge
Perilous Wilderness Escape
Tracked Through the Mountains
Abducted at Christmas
Uncovering Colorado Secrets

Visit the Author Profile page at LoveInspired.com.

Uncovering Colorado Secrets

RHONDA STARNES

LOVE INSPIRED SUSPENSE

INSPIRATIONAL ROMANCE

LOVE INSPIRED® SUSPENSE

INSPIRATIONAL ROMANCE

ISBN-13: 978-1-335-59809-7

Uncovering Colorado Secrets

Recycling programs
for this product may
not exist in your area.

Love Inspired
22 Adelaide St. West, 41st Floor
Toronto, Ontario M5H 4E3, Canada
www.LoveInspired.com

Printed in Lithuania

MIX
Paper | Supporting
responsible forestry
FSC® C021394

The Lord is my light and my salvation;
whom shall I fear? the Lord is the strength of my life;
of whom shall I be afraid?
—*Psalms* 27:1

For my daughter, Brittni, a military spouse and homeschooling mother of three. You are an amazing woman. I'm so proud to be your mom. I love you, Sunshine!

ONE

Bodyguard Adeline Scott struggled to pull herself out of a deep slumber. What had woken her? Was it one of the boys? Her eight-year-old nephews, Matthew and Josiah, hadn't slept through the night since their parents' deaths one week earlier. Their extended family—including Adeline's parents—had left after the funeral two days ago, and the boys had returned to their normal routine of school then soccer practice. She'd hoped this would be the night they'd all get a full night's rest.

Come on, wake up. Go check on the boys. She tried to coax her body into following the commands of her brain, but her eyelids felt like weighted blankets that refused to budge. Groaning, she rolled over and landed on the floor with a thump.

Jolted awake, she blinked a few times, until she could make out the shape of the mahogany desk across the room, illuminated only by the soft light of an antique-bronze desk lamp. She'd fallen asleep on the leather sofa in her brother-in-law's office. The small baby monitor sat on the side table where she'd placed it earlier while she'd sorted through her sister and brother-in-law's financial records. The green light on the monitor glowed, but no sound of the boys stirring came from it.

Matthew had been so indignant when she'd dug the baby monitor out of the storage tub labeled Baby Items in the garage. He'd kept saying, "We aren't babies, Aunt Addie. We don't need you monitoring us while we sleep or play in our room." The older twin by seven minutes, he'd always been more independent. The one who had remained stoic when they'd been told of their parents' automobile accident and who had promised Josiah that, as the big brother, he'd take care of him. It had taken a bit of convincing on her part, but Matthew had understood that guardianship was new to Adeline and the monitor was more for her sense of security than theirs. It had also helped that she'd agreed to use the monitor that resembled the two-way radio and not the one with the camera.

If the boys hadn't woken her, what had? Since her days as a child at summer camp, she'd trained herself to be a light sleeper so she didn't end up on the receiving end of a prank. Especially one like her cabinmates had pulled on Susie McLaughlin when they'd carried her—sound asleep, mattress and all—out of the cabin and put her on a table in the dining hall, where the counselors and other campers found her the next morning.

Using the sofa to brace herself, Adeline pushed to her feet, inched toward the open door and listened. Gunther wasn't barking. If an intruder was present, wouldn't the German shepherd have alerted her? Wait, what time was it? She pulled her phone out of her back pocket—1:37. The last thing she remembered was talking to her boss Lincoln Jameson about taking more time off to handle her sister's affairs. Addie checked her phone log. Lincoln had called her at a quarter to ten. After the call ended, she'd started printing bank statements, intending to bring Gunther in from the backyard once she'd finished. Her head had started hurting, so she had taken pain meds and sat on the sofa to wait for the printer to finish. That's when she must've fallen asleep.

Gunther was still outside! As if to punctuate her thoughts, he scraped the kitchen door that led to the backyard patio.

"Gunther, I'm sorry I forgot you, boy." She took off down the hall toward the back of the house. The big brute most likely would be mad at her and pout for the next few days. "Oh, Vanessa, how could you leave me with a temperamental German shepherd and two little boys who need a mother. You know I'm the least maternal person on the face of the earth."

Addie never would understand why her sister had named her guardian of Josiah and Matthew. And Gunther. If she could just get through the next month and a half, her nephews and their large dog would be off to Florida where they would spend the summer with their grandparents. And, if the boys adjusted well during that time, Addie would approach her mom and dad about taking over the guardianship responsibilities.

The sound of glass shattering reached her, and she picked up her pace. The overzealous dog had busted the glass patio door. She'd have to secure it the best she could for the night and call a repairman tomorrow. "Gunther, if you would—" The sound of the doorknob turning and the door opening halted her words. She ducked into the dining room, pressed her back against the wall and listened. Footsteps crunched on the broken glass, echoing the thump of her heart beating in her ears.

An intruder! Why wasn't Gunther growling? Had the intruder harmed him? Ugh. She needed her gun, which was upstairs in the small lockbox she stored it in when she was off duty. She'd hidden it on the top shelf of the closet in the guest room, out of reach of the children. Heavy footsteps clomped down the hall, the hardwood floors doing little to mask the sound. She grabbed one of the antique silver candlesticks her mother had gifted her sister as a wedding present. As a weapon, it wasn't a substitute for a gun, but it was better than nothing. Staying in the shadows, she inched toward the doorway and watched the intruder walk past. Standing well above her five-foot, ten-inch frame, she would put the man's height close to six-four. His broad shoulders indicated that he was a bodybuilder. Since she didn't know without a doubt she could subdue him, she couldn't risk confronting him and waking the boys. The last thing she needed was for one of them to come downstairs and be in harm's way.

Please, Lord, don't let the intruder go upstairs. Adeline mentally shook herself. What was she doing? She hadn't prayed in years, and she didn't intend to start now. The God she'd learned about in Bible class as a child had been a loving Father who'd wanted only to send blessings to His children. Even if she hadn't learned long ago that was a lie fabricated by people who'd needed something to believe in, she would have known it now. A loving God would not have taken her sister and brother-in-law, leaving her nephews orphans.

She needed to call for backup. Her normal, fiercely independent nature would not be in the best interest of the little boys sleeping upstairs. She pulled her phone out of her pocket, glanced at it, and when the screen lit up, pressed the device to her chest then covered it with both hands. Taking a few steps back, she sank deeper into the shadows.

The intruder stopped and half turned. A camo balaclava covered his face. Only his eyes were exposed by the hunting mask. His body blocked the small amount of light streaming through the blinds from the streetlight, so she couldn't make out the color of his eyes in the dark. She held her breath as she recalled images of the many people she'd met at the funeral, unable to place anyone who fit the build of the intruder.

After what felt like hours but, in reality, was only a matter of seconds, the intruder turned and continued on his way to the front of the house. He disappeared into Isaac's office.

Hopeful he was out of earshot, she pulled the phone away from her chest. "Adeline, answer me! If you can hear me, I'm on my way."

The candlestick slipped out of her hand and landed on the rug. "Linc?" she whispered into the phone.

"Yes. What's going on? You scared me. I'm—"

"There's an intruder," Adeline interjected in hushed tones. "He's in Isaac's office. I hear him opening drawers and things. I don't have my gun. And I don't know if I can make it upstairs to it, or the boys, without the intruder hearing me."

"I'm on my way. Did you call nine-one-one?"

"That's what I was about to do, but somehow I dialed you."

"I'm glad you did. I've texted Ryan. He'll report the break-in. I'll be there in eight minutes or less." Linc's authoritative voice soothed her nerves in a way she never would have thought possible.

"Okay." Adeline placed her hand on her chest and took a steadying breath. "I'll tiptoe down the hall and see if I think I can make it to my room to retrieve my gun."

"Are you sure—"

"Aunt Addie!" Josiah cried from the top of the stairs. "Where are you?"

"Josiah's awake. Hurry, Linc!" She darted out of the room and raced down the hall, desperate to reach her young nephew before the intruder could.

"Stay on the line with me," Linc ordered.

Adeline rounded the base of the staircase as the intruder stepped through the door of the office. She had to stop him from getting to Josiah before her. The memory of her nephews playing with her phone camera before bed rushed through her mind. Pulling her phone away from her ear, she pointed it at the dark figure.

"Say cheese." She snapped a photo, the flash momentarily blinding her adversary. A perfect roundhouse kick to his chest pushed him backward into the office. She slipped her phone into her pocket then darted up the stairs, thankful for the night-lights that guided her path.

Reaching her wide-eyed nephew, she scooped him up and tossed him over her shoulder the way firefighters carried victims out of a burning building.

"Put me down, Aunt Addie." Small legs flailed, and she tightened her grip.

"Hang tight, buddy."

Breathing heavily, she reached the landing and turned toward the boys' room. Matthew stood in the doorway, rubbing his eyes. "What's going on?"

"We're running from a bad guy," Josiah yelled.

"What bad guy? Where is he? I'll fight him." Matthew balled his fists and put them up like he was boxing.

When he made a move to go around her, she blocked his path and guided him back into the room. Then she kicked the door closed with her foot. Before she could turn to lock the door, she heard a click.

"I locked the door," Josiah declared.

"Thanks, buddy." She knelt to allow him to stand.

Big brown eyes stared back at her. "You're welcome."

"Come on, what are you guys doing? If there's a bad guy in the house, we have to fight him." Matthew tried to push Adeline aside.

"I know you want to fight the bad guy, but this isn't one of your video games. Help is on the way. We need to stay put until they get here." She grasped his shoulders and forced him to look at her. "Do you understand?"

A large bang sounded behind her, and the door rattled. Adeline jumped up to push the dresser in front of the door.

"Here, let me help." Matthew put his small hands beside hers.

"Me, too." Josiah squirmed his way between them.

The door frame splintered under the assault of the intruder. Adeline planted her feet firmly on the carpeted floor and leaned against the dresser, pushing with all her might. The heavy piece of furniture slid into place.

"I don't know who you are," she yelled, hugging her nephews to her and sinking to the floor. "But you need to leave. The police are on the way." *Please, Lord, let the police be on the way.*

"This isn't over," the intruder growled and hit the door one last time. "I will get what I came for, and I don't care how many dead bodies I have to leave behind."

Descending footsteps pounded on the stairs, and she puffed out a breath, willing her heart rate to slow. *Vanessa, what kind of mess have you and Isaac left me with?*

Lincoln Jameson pulled his sports car into the Coulters' driveway and put it into Park. He'd visited the home for the first time two days ago, following Vanessa and Isaac's memorial service. Darkness shrouded the residence. The streetlight casting an eerie glow on the front yard. He snatched his phone from the passenger seat. Linc could hear Adeline and her nephews talking quietly, but had given up trying to get their attention after he'd heard her tell the intruder to leave. Disconnecting the call, he slid the phone into his pocket. Then he opened the console, located a small flashlight, palmed his Glock and stepped out of the vehicle. Time to see if the intruder had followed orders or if the guy had hung around, waiting to attack an innocent woman and children.

Making his way to the side of the house, he discovered a German shepherd lying motionless by the patio. Kneeling, he placed his hand on the animal's chest. Good. The dog was still breathing.

The back door stood wide open. He stepped inside and broken glass crunched under his shoes. Linc gave his eyes a moment to adjust to the darkness as he listened. No sound. Clicking on the flashlight, he went from room to room on the first floor.

The office seemed to be the only room disturbed. Filing cabinet drawers hung open and files were askew, a few on the floor. Had the intruder made such a mess in the short time he'd been in the room? Or had Adeline left some of the clutter? She'd told him earlier that she would need a few more weeks off work to sort through her sister and brother-in-law's finances and get their estate in order. Had she ransacked the room? It didn't fit her normal behavior.

Although, he had to admit, even though she had worked for Protective Instincts for two years, he still didn't understand what made her tick. She was a proficient bodyguard, but she never wanted to connect with him or the rest of the staff. Even Bridget—his business partner's sister and the person everyone connected with—had not bridged a friendship with Adeline.

Downstairs was clear. Time to check out the upstairs. He inched his way up the steps. A splintered door to the right of the stairs caught his attention. Crossing to the door, he whispered, "I'm here, Adeline. You and the boys stay put until I clear the upstairs."

"Lincoln! Be careful."

"Will do." The upstairs consisted of a master suite, a bathroom and two smaller bedrooms—the one his employee and her nephews were holed up inside and a guest room. Linc had finished clearing the last room when sirens sounded.

He turned on the hall light and rapped his knuckles on the boys' bedroom door. "All clear. You can come out."

The door opened and Adeline stepped through the doorway with one nephew hiding behind her while the other one stood tall beside her, his shoulders squared. What was it she had told him about the boys' personalities? Matthew wanted to be the man of the house, believing it was his responsibility as the oldest to take his dad's place, and Josiah was more emotionally fragile, afraid to let her out of his sight for fear he'd lose her, too.

"Sounds like the police have arrived," he addressed

Adeline. "Maybe the boys should wait in their room while you answer questions."

"I'm no—"

Adeline knelt beside her nephew. "He's right, Matthew. I need to answer the police officers' questions without distraction. The best way you can help me is to stay upstairs with Josiah."

"But—"

"Yes, Matthew. Stay with me." Josiah peeked around his aunt's shoulder, a pleading look on his face. "I don't want to be alone if the bad guy comes back."

The stoic nephew looked like he might argue, but then he wrapped his arm around his brother and guided him back into the room. "Okay, but you have to follow my instructions. We'll leave the light off, but we'll get our Nerf guns and be ready if he comes back."

"No, Matthew. I don't want to be in the dark. We need to see the bad guy coming."

Matthew sighed. "We'll leave the closet light on, but that's all. If we leave the room light on, he'll know we're in here."

Adeline stood and watched the boys, her hand covering her mouth and her shoulders shaking. Linc couldn't tell if she was laughing or crying. *Lord, don't let her fall apart on me. I don't know how to console a crying woman.*

The bedroom door closed and the lock clicked into place. "We're okay, Aunt Addie. You can go talk to the police. I'll keep Josiah safe."

"Thank you, Matthew. I'll come back upstairs as quickly as I can." She turned and faced him, her brown eyes shining, and shook her head. "I don't know what I'm going to do with that child for the next six weeks. He's so determined to be an adult and has showed no emotion through all of this."

Linc placed his hand on the small of her back and turned her toward the stairs. "All boys grieve in their own way. If you're still concerned after he's had a little more time, you can seek the guidance of an expert. But first, let's let the police in so we can try to figure out who ransacked your brother-in-law's office."

As if on cue, someone knocked on the front door. "Police!"

"Coming." She squared her shoulders and, with an expression much like the one he'd seen on Josiah's face, headed down the stairs.

Linc didn't know how to tell her he was as worried about her as she was about her nephews. His by-the-book employee seemed to be in over her head, and the added threat of an intruder looking for something the dead brother-in-law had left behind might be more than even she could handle. His employee would soon understand the military credo of no man—or in this case, woman—left behind, as well as the marine's credo *Semper fidelis*. Always Faithful. Both were mottos he lived by. Stamped into his heart and soul during his many tours of duty. He would not leave her side until he knew, without a doubt, she and the boys were safe from harm.

TWO

"It was probably a random break-in. You startled them with your presence. They won't return." The older officer, who was most likely biding his time until retirement, closed his small notebook and peered at Adeline. "We'll file a report, though."

"My presence didn't startle him." Having worked for ten years as a police officer before applying for the position at Protective Instincts, she resented the older man's dismissive attitude. "You saw the bedroom door. He tried to harm us."

"Yes, ma'am. However, the moment you told him the police were on their way, he ran away. If he'd really wanted to hurt you, he wouldn't have taken off until he heard our sirens."

"So that's it? You're going to file a report that it was a random break-in and—"

Linc put an arm around her, halting her words. "Thank you, Officers. We appreciate you responding to the call so quickly."

Adeline turned to him, and he subtly shook his head, a pleading look in his eyes. The cop had annoyed her, and in the same way she'd witnessed Linc resolve conflict in the workplace, he was attempting to deflect the potential conflict between her and the officer. She blew out a breath. Okay, fine. Besides, the sooner the police left, the sooner Adeline could get down to business and figure out what the intruder had been looking for. She turned toward the man and his partner. "Yes, thank you for the quick response."

"All in a day's work, ma'am." The annoying officer tipped his hat and walked out the front door.

His partner, a younger man in his early- to midthirties, followed behind with a half smile. "Try not to worry, ma'am. Break-ins in homes where the homeowners have recently passed are not uncommon. Unfortunately, there are people out there who scour the obituaries, looking for homes to target. I'm sure finding the home occupied startled the intruder, and he'll think twice about returning. But as a precaution, we'll drive by every hour tonight."

"Thank you." Adeline closed the door behind the officer then turned and glared at Linc. "You interrupted me."

"I know. I'm sorry." He held up his hands, in surrender. "It wasn't my place to interfere, but I could read that guy's body language. Nothing you said was going to change his mind. Besides, you'd already told him about the threat the intruder made."

She sighed. "You're right. It's just frustrating not to be taken seriously." The officer's attitude shouldn't have surprised her. There had been several cops like him on the police force in Dallas, too. One of many reasons she'd left her job there. That and the fact that the officer who'd caused the death of the man she'd loved had been allowed to retire and draw his pension without any kind of reprimand.

"I get it. But, really, what else can they do at two in the

morning to catch the guy? You don't have a description, other than muscular and tall. The photo, while an ingenious way to escape, had given no clues to the guy's identity since the balaclava covered everything but his eyes."

"I guess." An idea struck. "What about footprints? They could have taken photos of the backyard."

"And if they had, they wouldn't have known which ones belonged to the intruder. You had more than fifty people in that backyard two days ago, following the memorial. The patio and yard are covered in prints. Including mine."

Why did her boss always have to be so logical? "You know, it's annoying when you're right all the time."

Linc pressed his lips together and shrugged.

Adeline shook her head then gathered her hair and slipped the ever-present hair tie off her wrist, securing her wavy brown locks into a messy bun. "I need to check on the boys then board up the back door." She turned to Lincoln. "Thank you for coming."

"I'll stick around, if it's okay with you." He planted his feet firmly and squared his shoulders, as if he was ready to stand his ground.

She stood silently for a few moments before agreeing. It would be nice if he stayed until they secured the door. Maybe then she wouldn't feel so vulnerable. "Okay. Thanks. You go look in the garage for something to board up the back door. I'll meet you in the kitchen." Adeline jogged up a few stairs, stopped and turned back to him, a frightened expression on her face. "I forgot about Gunther."

"German shepherd?"

"That's right. How'd—"

"I found him in the backyard, unconscious." He held up his hand when she gasped. "He was breathing and didn't have any obvious wounds. The intruder probably gave him something to knock him out. Go check on the boys. I'll take care of Gunther before I fix the door."

There he went, taking charge again. *Let it go. It's okay to relinquish control sometimes.*

Adeline plastered a smile on her face. "Thank you." She turned and sprinted up the stairs.

Twenty minutes later, she walked into the kitchen to discover Lincoln attaching a sheet of plywood over the glass door.

"Sorry it took me so long," Adeline said once the whirring sound of the power tool stopped. "I had to agree to let Josiah sleep in my room, and I couldn't sneak back down here until he fell asleep." She stopped in the middle of the room. "Wow. I didn't expect you to be finished so quickly."

"Your brother-in-law was apparently a handyman who enjoyed doing repairs around the house. The small storage area in the garage has a chest with every imaginable tool and there are sheets of plywood and a variety of boards leaned against the back wall." He placed the battery-operated screwdriver back into its hard plastic case, snapped the lid closed and smiled at her. "I'm glad Josiah is sleeping. Is Matthew asleep, also?"

She bit her lip and shook her head. "No. He's sitting outside my room with his Nerf gun. Guarding his brother. I left a pillow and a blanket beside him. If he falls asleep, I'll try to move him to the bed without waking him."

Her heart ached for her nephew, who'd gone from a fun-loving kid to a miniature adult overnight. At the funeral, he'd stood next to his parents' caskets like a soldier at full attention. Greeting each guest with a handshake, he'd echoed her sentiments, saying, "Thank you for coming," to every person in attendance. A tear slipped out of the corner of her eye. "Uh…um." She cleared her throat and turned from her employer's scrutinizing gaze to dab the moisture away.

Gunther lay on the floor mat in front of the sink, a bowl of water nearby. She crossed over and got on her knees before the German shepherd. He lifted his head a few inches and pinned her with sad eyes, then moaned and laid his head back down.

"Shouldn't we take him to the animal hospital?" Adeline asked as she stroked Gunther's fur. "I don't think Matthew and Josiah could handle losing another family member right now."

"I did a video call with Grace Bradshaw, a veterinarian from Blackberry Falls. She doesn't think the intruder poisoned Gunther. She said it was more likely that he gave him something to put him to sleep. But she told me symptoms to look for, and if he exhibits any of them, I promise to take him to the emergency hospital." Linc knelt beside her and scratched between the shepherd's ears. "He's going to be fine. Aren't you, boy?"

She frowned, recalling a conversation she'd had with Bridget, the bodyguard she'd replaced at Protective Instincts. "Blackberry Falls. Isn't that the small town where Ryan and Bridget grew up? Bridget had made it sound like a dull place where nothing exciting ever happened. Do you really think a vet from there would have much experience with dogs being poisoned?"

"Grace was a highly sought-after veterinary surgeon who lived and worked in Denver for over a decade before taking over her family veterinary clinic in Blackberry Falls. I promise you, if she felt Gunther was in a life-threatening situation, she would have told me to get him to the hospital." He turned to face her, his brow creased in concern. "But, it's your call. If you think we should take Gunther to the animal hospital to be examined, we will. However, you're not going without me, and I'm not going without you and the boys. So, if that's what you think we should do, we'll wake the boys and go."

Heat spread up her neck and she fought the urge to squirm under his gaze. The employees at Protective Instincts knew Lincoln Jameson's take-charge nature well, and Adeline had experienced his things-will-be-done-my-way attitude multiple times. When he'd insisted on staying behind to help, she'd expected him to take over. That had bothered her, but this side of him she'd never seen before unnerved her even more.

Lincoln waited. And the seconds ticked by. Adeline pushed a loose strand of her dark brown hair behind her ear then shoved to her feet and paced. He stood, leaned against the counter and watched.

The seconds turned to minutes. And he continued to wait, which was hard for someone used to being in charge. Through the years, first as a marine and now as a business owner of a security firm, he'd been in many positions where he'd had to make quick decisions, some being a matter of life and death. He was used to giving orders and having them followed. Waiting in a stranger's kitchen for one of his employees to make the call on the next move was a novel experience—and not one he liked. But this was Adeline's family, and it had to be her call.

Finally, she stopped in the middle of the room and turned to him, a torn expression on her face. "I don't know what to do. Help me."

Before he could examine his actions, he crossed the room and pulled her into a hug. "It's okay. You've been through a lot in the past week. Losing your sister and her husband and finding out you're the guardian of their children. Then to have the home broken into and your and your nephews' lives put in danger... I'd be more worried if you didn't feel overwhelmed."

She wrapped her arms around his waist and wept, releasing all the stress of the past week.

If her at-home persona was anything like the one she exhibited at work, she most likely had been so focused on her nephews that she hadn't even allowed herself to grieve the loss of her sister. Linc wrapped her close and stroked her hair, wanting to provide comfort but not do anything that would disrupt what he imagined was a much-needed release of emotions. After a few moments, she stepped out of his arms. The action leaving a feeling of emptiness he pushed to the back of his mind and refused to assess.

Adeline crossed to the sink, tore a paper towel off the roll, wiped her eyes and stared out the kitchen window into the backyard. "I'm sorry. You must think I'm a frail female, falling apart about whether or not to take a pet to the vet." She turned and faced him. "I'll understand if you decide I'm not good bodyguard material and want to terminate me."

Anger bubbled up inside him. Did she really think he was so uncaring that he couldn't show sympathy to someone in pain? He clinched his teeth, and a muscle twitched in his jaw. Inhaling deeply, he counted to five then exhaled. "I'm sorry if I've done anything to give you the impression your job would be on the line if you displayed emotions."

She opened her mouth to speak, and he rushed to continue, "I think you are one of the best bodyguards we've ever hired. You've never questioned an order or complained about long hours. And, once you get things figured out here, your job will be waiting for you…in whatever capacity you need. Protective Instincts is more than a business. It's a family. We take care of our own. And if your schedule needs to shift to more of a nine-to-five situation because you've become the single parent of two boys, we'll figure it out. Got it?"

Her eyes clouded, but she nodded. "Thank you."

"You're welcome. Now, what—" The sound of Gunther lapping up water drew his attention. The German shepherd hunched over the water bowl, drinking as if he'd not had water in days.

"Gunther!" Adeline sank to the floor and wrapped her arms around his neck, burying her face in his fur.

Linc looked heavenward. *Thank You, Lord.*

"I guess your friend was right. Please, thank her for me." Adeline smiled at him.

He nodded. "Now that we know Gunther is fine, do you want to look for clues in the office?"

She looked at the stove clock. "It's almost four."

"So? What time do the boys have to be woken up for school?"

"The bus runs at seven. I thought I'd get them up around six-twenty."

"Okay. If you want to grab a two-hour nap, I'll stretch

out on the sofa in the living room, and we'll start in the office after the boys leave for school."

Her eyes widened. "You're staying the night?"

"I already told you, I'm not leaving until I know you and the boys are safe." He gently grasped her by the shoulders, pulled her to her feet and led her out of the kitchen and down the hall, Gunther right on their heels.

"Yes, but—"

"No arguments. I promise to try not to force my opinions on you and not to overstep in making decisions for this family—like whether to take a beloved pet to the vet. However, I do not, for one minute, believe this was a random break-in by someone who had searched the obituaries, and I refuse to leave you to deal with this alone." He stopped in the entry and turned to face her. "We can stand here and continue to debate this issue or you can go upstairs, check on your nephews and get a few hours of sleep."

The look on her face led him to believe she was going to argue with him, but then she pressed her lips together, nodded and crossed to the keypad beside the front door. She entered a series of numbers and engaged the alarm. "The sofa in the office is more comfortable for sleeping than the one in the living room. There's a pillow and a throw blanket already in there, too," she said as she headed up the stairs.

He smiled, knowing how hard it was for her to accept help and appreciating that she trusted him. Returning to the kitchen, he double-checked the security bolt on the back door then verified all the windows were secure. Then he turned off the lights and went from room to room, repeating the process.

Once back at the front door, he looked a little more

closely at the security system. Why hadn't Adeline set the alarm earlier? Was it because Gunther had been outside and she'd wanted to wait until he was back indoors? If so, he really needed to have a talk with her about safety. Even though it would mean disengaging and reengaging the alarm multiple times, the security measure could help keep her and the boys protected. Or at least give them a few moments' warning that danger was present so they could take action to hide.

Dimming the entryway light, he left it on low and went into the office. Stepping over files strewn around the room, he crossed to the desk and clicked the button to turn off the lamp, casting the office in darkness, the only light coming through the open door.

Walking around the desk, he moved the blinds to check the window latches and froze. All the windows in the house were locked, except for this one. Even though Adeline had not activated the security alarm, there was no way he thought the unlocked windows in the office was a coincidence. The intruder must have unlocked them before he left. Clicking the lock into place, Linc froze. Two white wires stuck out haphazardly. The intruder had cut the security alarm on the window.

Automobile headlights flashed on an oak tree in the side yard, and Linc moved to the front window to peer out. A police car drove slowly down the street. The young officer had kept his word. Movement in an upstairs window in the house across the street caught Linc's attention. A dark figure stood, looking directly at the Coulters' house. When the police cruiser drew closer, the figure moved out of sight, a small corner of the curtain still open as they watched the car drive past.

   Was it a case of a nosy neighbor, or did the intruder live across the street? Linc would have to investigate this new discovery first thing in the morning, right after Ryan checked out the security system and possibly installed a better one.

THREE

"Why is that man sleeping on Daddy's couch?" Josiah asked, heading for the office door.

Adeline caught the inquisitive child by his upper arm and turned him to face her. "That's Mr. Jameson, my boss. Remember, he came by last night after that man broke in?"

"But why is he sleeping here?"

"Because men are supposed to protect women," Matthew replied through gritted teeth as he shoved his arms through his backpack. "Guess he failed to notice there is a man of the house here to protect Aunt Addie. Except…" He turned and glared at her. "I can't do my job if you insist on treating me like a baby. I was fine sleeping in the hall with my gun. You didn't have to carry me to my bed."

Curling her hands into fists at her sides, Adeline dug her nails into her palms and fought the urge to sweep him into her arms and tell him he didn't have to throw away his childhood. That she was the adult and she would take care of him and Josiah. *If only temporarily.* She pushed the thought out of her head. One issue at a time. "I thought you might rest better in your bed. Besides, the police were adamant that they didn't think the guy would return, so I knew we would be fine."

"Then why did *he* sleep over?" Matthew jerked his head toward the office.

Lincoln shifted from his back onto his side, and Adeline suspected her boss was awake and listening to the conversation. "Because he's going to help me get the back door repaired." She swallowed. "Where the intruder broke in last night."

"I could do that." Matthew planted his tiny fist on his hips. "I helped Dad with repairs all the time."

"Yeah, me, too," Josiah said, mimicking Matthew's stance.

She knelt, so she'd be at eye level with her nephews. "I know you could help. Both of you. Only, you've missed several days of school already, and if you miss many more, it will be harder to catch up on all your work." Adeline smiled and placed a hand on each twin's cheek. "What if we go to the lumber store this weekend to get the supplies to build you guys a fort? Then, for your birthday next month, you can invite a couple of friends for a sleepover in the backyard, complete with s'mores." Why had she opened her big mouth and promised them a fort? They'd put all that work into a project they'd only get to enjoy for a short while if they moved to Florida to live with their grandparents.

"Oh, boy! Yeah!" Josiah threw his arms around her neck and she hugged him tightly.

This was why. She wanted to bring these little boys as much joy as possible in the short time that she had them. Adeline might not have maternal yearnings like most women her age, but she loved her nephews and would do everything she could to keep them safe and make their time together fun.

Matthew watched the exchange with a frown on his face. She met his gaze, and he shrugged. "Okay. I guess. But tell your boss I can protect this house without him." Then he tugged Josiah's arm. "Come on, or we'll miss the bus."

Matthew's desire to be grown and skip his childhood broke her heart, but there wasn't anything she could do about it at the moment.

Adeline pushed to her feet, grabbed the stack of thank-you cards she'd written to the people who had sent flowers or delivered food and followed the boys out the front door. She was on the bottom step of the porch when Matthew stopped and frowned at her. "Aunt Addie, I told you, Mom let us walk to the bus stop alone."

The memory of a phone conversation with her sister back in August flitted through her mind. Vanessa had giggled as she'd recounted to Adeline how she'd let the twins think they were walking to the bus stop alone when in reality she watched their every step.

I don't want to be a helicopter mom, but there are too many stories in the news about missing children. Letting Matthew and Josiah feel like they're walking to the bus stop alone, even though I'm outside putting mail in the box or walking to a neighbor's house on the pretense of borrowing something, is my way of trying to help them have a sense of independence while keeping eyes on them, soothing my own anxiety.

She smiled and held up her hand, displaying the envelopes she'd grabbed off the entryway table. Stamped and ready to go into the box. "I know. I'm just putting the thank-you cards into the mailbox." Adeline stepped around the boys and continued down the walkway. "Have a great day, guys."

"You, too, Aunt Addie," Josiah yelled cheerfully.

Matthew shrugged and continued toward the bus stop at the end of the block, stopping midway to look over his shoulder. Fortunately, she'd already taken up a position behind the big maple tree in the corner of the front yard. When he didn't see her, a big smile spread across his face and he continued on with a little more bounce in his step.

Someone came up behind her and she jumped. A hand clamped over her mouth, suppressing her scream.

"Shh. It's just me," Lincoln whispered into her ear.

Taking a couple of slow breaths to ease her heart thundering inside her chest, she turned to glare at him. "What were you thinking, frightening me like that?"

"I'm sorry." He stepped back. "When you jumped, I was afraid you'd scream, giving away your hiding place… I only wanted to watch the boys get onto the bus safely."

"The boys!" She turned back just in time to see Matthew's backpack disappear through the bus doors.

The bus headed in their direction. Adeline scooted around the side of the tree. Lincoln mimicked her movement, and they both pressed close to the tree trunk. She was acutely aware of her boss's presence, his breath on her neck as he crowded close to her. Her heart fluttered. *Stop it, Addie.*

She didn't have time for some schoolgirl crush on her boss. Besides, she had learned long ago that men rarely wanted tough, independent women. They wanted a woman who needed protecting. And Adeline would rather live alone the rest of her life than be a simpering, weak female.

The wind blew a strand of Adeline's hair across Lincoln's face. The scent of her citrus shampoo wafted around him, and he fought the urge to bury his face in her silken locks and inhale. *Get a grip, man. Remember your vow to remain a bachelor. It wouldn't be fair to ask any woman to accept you and your chosen career.*

Even if he didn't have strong convictions about the unfairness of someone in his line of work marrying and having children, he'd never date an employee. He could only blame the proximity they had found themselves in for the sudden overwhelming awareness he felt toward Adeline.

Lincoln focused on the bus. Once it turned out of sight, he stepped away from the tree, putting as much distance as possible between them.

He cleared his throat and looked up to meet her gaze. "I'm sorry I startled you earlier. The way you handled Matthew's need to be a miniature man of the house was amazing."

"So, you weren't asleep." She grinned at him with one eyebrow raised. "I thought as much."

"Well, no. But, in all fairness, I didn't do it to be deceitful. If I had let you know I was awake, Matthew probably would have started lecturing me on all the reasons he was the *man of the house*, and he and Josiah may have missed the bus."

Laughter bubbled out of her. She pressed her lips together, covered her mouth with one hand and held her side with the other.

"What's so funny?" His question only encouraged more laughter. He didn't understand why him playing opossum was so hilarious. "Fine. I'll wait until you've finished laughing at me to tell you what I discovered last night."

His statement had the sobering effect he'd hoped for,

and she gulped a few steadying breaths. A few seconds later, she faced him, fully composed.

"What did you find?"

He crossed his arms and leaned against the tree. "You first? Why did you think it was funny that I pretended to be asleep?"

One corner of her mouth lifted and a dimple appeared in her cheek. "You've always been a take-charge kind of guy. It's amusing to see you afraid of a confrontation with an eight-year-old."

"Oh, come on. I wouldn't say I'm afraid of him, but you've got to admit, your nephew is one intimidating little dude. He's eight going on eighty. I've never met anyone his age who acts less like a kid than he does." He cocked his head. "Has he always been like that, or is it something new that's come out in his personality since his parents' deaths?"

She turned and headed across the lawn to the porch. "Matthew has always been more serious than Josiah. I'm not sure if it's because he's the oldest or just a personality trait. He always preferred reading in his dad's office while Isaac worked or helping Vanessa in the kitchen while she cooked. Josiah, on the other hand, would be in the family room playing a video game or outside building a fort."

"Don't you think he's being too stoic?"

Adeline paused midway up the front steps and pinned him with a cool stare. Linc regretted his words instantly. He'd overstepped, again. "I'm sorry. You know the boys. I don't. If this is Matthew's typical behavior, I'm sure there isn't anything to worry about."

"While I hate to admit it, you probably have as good of an understanding of the boys and their behaviors as I do, if not better. Remember, I lived in Dallas the first almost seven years of their lives, so I was only around for brief visits." A deep sigh escaped her. "I'll call their pediatrician and get a referral for counseling for both boys. Thank you for pointing out the need. I should have thought of it sooner."

After hiring Adeline to replace Bridget when she moved to Tennessee to marry FBI profiler Sawyer Eldridge and open a second branch of Protective Instincts, Linc had noticed how much Adeline was Bridget's opposite. Where Bridget was a petite redhead with a bubbly personality, Adeline was a leggy brunette with a no-nonsense, take-charge approach to life. He sensed she had a deep-seated need for independence, similar to that of her young nephew. Maybe Matthew had inherited some of his aunt's personality. If so, Linc imagined the boy would grow up to do great things one day.

"You have a pensive look on your face." Adeline broke into his thoughts. "Are you ready to tell me what you discovered last night?"

"Yes. But let's step indoors, away from prying eyes." He followed her inside. Once the door was closed, he pointed to the security keypad. "I noticed you set the alarm last night before going upstairs to bed. Why didn't you set it earlier in the evening? I would have thought, with your training, that you would keep the alarm system active at all times, especially since I don't see any motion detectors and the alarms are only on the exterior doors and the windows."

"But I *did* activate the alarm. After the boys' soccer practice, we stopped at a fast-food restaurant to grab chicken nuggets and burgers. When we got home, Matthew fed

Gunther while I plated our food. We all ate, and then the boys went upstairs to get ready for bed. I let Gunther outside and reactivated the alarm before going upstairs to read the boys a bedtime story. By this time, it was getting late, but Gunther had been stuck inside most of the day, so I decided to let him stay out for an extra hour while I sorted through the files in the office. But I fell asleep and—" She gasped and her eyes rounded. "The alarm didn't go off when the intruder entered the house. He disabled it…"

"Or he knew the code," they said in unison.

"Well, the intruder knew about the alarm system. He took the time to unlock a window in the office and cut the wires leading to the sensor."

She darted into the office.

"What are you doing?" he asked, following close behind.

"Something strange is going on here. The answer is in this room somewhere, and I intend to find it."

He put a hand on her arm, halting her from opening the filing cabinet. "Before we get lost, falling down rabbit holes that may or may not lead to answers, can you tell me anything about the neighbor across the street?" He guided her to the window and pointed to the house where he'd seen the person last night.

"That's Mrs. McCall's house. Why?"

"What do you know about Mrs. McCall? Does she live alone?"

"Yes, Vanessa said her husband passed away the year she and Isaac bought this house. The twins were two. Mrs. McCall never had children of her own, and she kind of adopted Vanessa's family, becoming an honorary grandmother to the boys. Again, why are you asking?"

"I noticed someone peeking out of an upstairs window

when the police drove past last night. It was obvious they were trying not to be spotted, so I wondered if they could be the intruder." He rubbed his chin. "If she's such a close family friend, would your sister have given Mrs. McCall the passcode to the alarm?"

"I'm sure she did. Mrs. McCall always brought in the mail and checked on things when they went on vacations." Adeline frowned. "The intruder was a man. I told you that."

"I know. Doesn't mean he was working alone, but I'm not saying Mrs. McCall is involved. However, I'd still like to talk to her. Even if she isn't behind the break-in, she may have seen something."

That was possible. Adeline had caught the woman watching the house many times in the past week. She'd brushed it off as a grieving friend keeping an eye out on the boys who were under the care of their single aunt. But what if there was more to the constant vigil the elder woman had put into practice over the past week? Could Mrs. McCall know something about the break-in or the mysterious circumstances of the accident that had caused Vanessa's and Isaac's deaths? There was only one way to find out.

"You know, I think it's time I pay Mrs. McCall a visit and thank her for being such a good neighbor to my sister all these years," she said, heading for the door. "Come on. I'll introduce you and let her know not to be concerned if she sees you here over the next few days. I'll say I'm working from home while I adjust to my new guardianship role."

"Sounds like a good plan." Lincoln followed her out of the house and down the steps.

The neighborhood was quiet, most of the homeowners having already left for work. It hit her how alone she was out here in the suburbs. She didn't know any of the neighbors, other than Mrs. McCall, whom she doubted would be much help in an emergency. Even the police response had been slower here than in the city. Maybe she should have moved the boys into her condo. At least her building had controlled access, and even if someone got past the locked entrance and doorman, she trusted her security system. If that failed, with a police station on the next block, she was confident a police officer would be on her doorstep in three minutes flat.

Adeline hated to think about what might have happened last night if she hadn't accidentally phoned Lincoln. "Thank you for coming so quickly last night."

"You're welcome." He smiled. "Now, if you're ready, let's go see what Mrs. McCall can tell us. Since you know her and I don't, I'll follow your lead."

He would follow her lead. She never thought she'd hear those words come out of her boss's mouth in relation to her. In the two-years that she'd been employed by Protective Instincts, she'd figured out that Ryan was the "laid-back tech guru" half of the owner equation and Linc was the "take charge get things done" half. It seemed to work well as her bosses complemented each other's management style, but she also knew whenever Linc was involved in an assignment, things were going to be done his way. She'd assumed that trait carried over to his personal life, too, and he'd be the same even if the situation he was involved in wasn't an assignment.

Maybe she'd misjudged Lincoln Jameson. She'd have

to see if he meant what he'd said when they were talking to Mrs. McCall.

She nodded, looked both ways and headed across the street. An engine roared to life and a black sports car pulled away from the curb halfway up the block, headed in their direction. Adeline paused to allow the car to pass, but it swerved into the left lane, increased speed and headed straight for her. The driver was going to hit them!

FOUR

Adeline stood transfixed, frozen in fear, as the sports car with tinted windows barreled toward her. Her brain screamed, *Move, now!* But her legs forgot how. A muscular arm snaked around her waist and jerked her backward. The breeze created by the car as it roared past—missing her by mere inches—blew her hair into her face. Lincoln pulled her close and dove into the yard. Their arms and legs tangled as they rolled behind the maple tree where they'd hidden from the twins earlier.

"Are you okay?" he asked breathlessly.

The pounding of her heart in her throat made it impossible to form words, so she bobbed her head instead.

Tires screeched and the smell of burnt rubber crinkled her nose. Adeline pushed to her feet and peered around the tree as the sports car reversed then stopped even with their hiding place. She reached for the Glock she'd hidden in her waistband. The holster was empty. Scanning the area, she located the revolver on the pavement only a few feet behind the sports car.

"Don't even think about it," Lincoln whispered in her ear, his breath warm on her neck. "You'd be dead before you reached it."

"You're right." She watched the vehicle sit there, taunting them. "Mrs. McCall is peeking through the curtains. Maybe she called the police."

Adeline glanced at the revolver in her boss's hand. "Are you going to use that, or are we going to stay trapped here all day?"

"I'm biding my time." His eyes never wavered from the car idling twenty feet from them.

"But you could easily shoot out his tires from this distance."

"And the police show up. The guy says he didn't mean to almost run us over and stopped to check on us. At which point, I shot at him. Then I go to jail and you and the boys are left vulnerable to another attack."

He was right, but it was frustrating to be taunted by the unknown assailant sitting behind the curtain of tinted windows. What was the guy waiting for? He had them trapped. If he had a weapon, why not open fire? Was he enjoying his little game of cat and mouse? The motor revved, as if he could read her thoughts and wanted her to know who was in charge.

The sports car backed up to the spot where Adeline's revolver rested and the driver's door inched open.

"No!"

Before the driver could grab the gun, Ryan's silver king-cab truck with built-in toolboxes along both sides of the bed turned onto the street from the opposite direction near the school bus stop.

The sports car door banged shut and the driver tooted the horn and raced down the street.

"The cavalry has arrived." Linc stepped around the tree, his weapon at the ready.

She darted to her gun, Linc close on her heels.

Ryan pulled up beside where they stood on the sidewalk. The passenger's-side window rolled down. "What's going on?"

"That driver tried to run us over." Lincoln jerked open the passenger door, hopped in, slammed it and shouted, "Follow them!"

"Wait!" Adeline yelled as Ryan did a U-turn and sped away.

Lincoln stuck his head out the window. "Go inside and stay put. And call the police."

How dare he dismiss her like that! In addition to being a former police officer, she was a highly skilled bodyguard, trusted to protect innocent people on a daily basis. She turned toward the house, her steps faltering. A highly trained security specialist would have had their weapon in a shoulder holster so it was more secure and the perp wouldn't have been able to almost take it. Maybe the male counterparts she'd worked with through the years, who'd seemed to question her ability, had been right. Perhaps it was time she sought employment in an office some place. Maybe in Florida, so she could be near the boys when they moved in with her parents. She had no doubt, once they heard the events that had transpired since they left, her parents would agree she wasn't parental material and would willingly raise the boys.

"Addie, dear!" Mrs. McCall waved at her from across the street. "The police are on their way. Wait with me, in case that car comes back."

For a split second, Adeline wondered if it was wise to defy her boss. *Stop it! He isn't the boss here.* This wasn't an assignment for Protective Instincts. It was her family— her life—being targeted.

"Coming Mrs. McCall."

* * *

"You know, you really shouldn't have done that."

"What?" Linc glanced at Ryan then turned his attention back to the sports car they were chasing. "Hurry. He's turning right on Monroe Street."

Ryan took the turn a little fast and Linc grabbed the hold bar to keep from sliding across the seat. "If he makes it to the interstate, we'll lose him. Maybe—"

"Maybe, let me do the driving," Ryan stated flatly. "You call nine-one-one and give them the guy's license plate number."

Linc fished his phone out of his back pocket. "I hope the officers who respond to this call are more helpful than the officers last night. They dismissed Adeline's concerns."

"Kind of like you just did?"

"What are you talking about?"

"Ordering her to call the police and wait inside when she wanted to come with us."

"So you think she should stand around outside and wait for the guy to come back and finish the job?"

"Don't get testy with me. Remember, I'm your friend." Ryan maneuvered around a garbage truck and merged onto the interstate, trying to stick close to the vehicle they were following. "Sometimes, you just get caught up in situations and forget you're not the one in charge."

"But I'm the—" *Boss.* No, he wasn't. Not this time. "Oh, boy."

Ryan laughed. "Exactly. Now, make that call and give a description of the vehicle while I figure out the best route to get us back to Adeline."

"But we didn't catch the guy yet." Lincoln searched

the sea of vehicles fighting their way through the early morning gridlock of commuters.

"You won't find him. He's gone. It's easier for the driver in a compact car to weave in and out of this traffic than for someone like me in a large truck." Ryan shrugged.

Linc sighed and called in the vehicle's description, complete with the license number. Then he slumped against the seat and contemplated his actions from earlier. How would he have felt if she'd dismissed him like that, especially if he'd been the one being targeted? Looked like he owed his employee… No. In this situation, she wasn't his employee, but they weren't quite friends either. He wasn't sure what word would describe their relationship. Whatever they were to each other, one thing was for sure: he owed her an apology.

Ten minutes later, they turned onto the Coulters' street, and Linc sat straighter. A police car sat in Mrs. McCall's driveway, and Adeline stood in the middle of the road, talking to a female officer, while Mrs. McCall stood on the sidewalk, speaking to a male officer. "Let me out by the sidewalk. Then you can pull into the driveway and start unloading the security equipment."

"You got it, boss."

He blew out a breath and tried again. "I'm sorry. Ryan, please, let me out by the sidewalk."

"Sure thing, bro." Ryan grinned.

Biting back the smile that threatened, Linc clapped his best friend on the shoulder. "Thank you. For always being straightforward with me."

"Anytime," Ryan replied, as he stopped the truck.

Linc took a good look at his friend, the man who, even though he'd never made it to the altar with Linc's sister, Jessica, would always be his brother. They had been through a great deal in the past eight years, but Jessica's murderer was in prison and Ryan had found a new love. The dark circles under Ryan's eyes had disappeared and the creases in his forehead had softened. "You know, you look about ten years younger. Seems like finding Hadley and Sophia and learning to relax has been good for you."

"Ah, come on, man. Don't go getting mushy just because I told you to stop being so hard-nosed." Ryan chuckled. "But you're right. Love has a way of putting things into perspective. And softening a person."

Was that what love did to a person? Lincoln had no doubt he could use a little softening around the edges. Maybe that was why well-meaning family members and friends often hinted he should look into joining an online dating service. Should he? He couldn't see himself doing that. Besides, in his line of work, the danger of injury or death was too great. Linc didn't want to have children who could one day end up orphans like Matthew and Josiah. Some people weren't meant to have a family of their own. Oh, well, being a bachelor also had its perks. He just couldn't think of any at the moment. Getting out of the truck, he jogged over to Adeline.

She looked up as he came near, and her brown eyes widened with hope and anticipation. "Tell me you got him."

"I wish I could but, unfortunately, I can't. However, we got his license plate number and phoned it in."

This sparked the female officer's attention. "You got a plate number? Come with me and we'll run it."

Linc followed close behind the officer, but then, realizing he was taking over again, slowed his steps to allow

Adeline to catch up. When they reached the police cruiser, the officer was already settled into the front seat and on her computer. He rattled off the plate number and she entered it into the database.

A few seconds later, she looked up with a frown. "Well, folks, it seems the plates are stolen. That number comes back registered to a yellow Volkswagen Beetle driven by a nineteen-year-old female." She stepped out of the cruiser. "We'll pay her a visit to make sure she isn't connected to the incident, but chances are, she's not even aware her plates have been taken."

The officer's partner walked over to them with Mrs. McCall. "Looks like we're done here. If any of you remember anything else, call the station."

After the officers left, Mrs. McCall turned and eyed them. "I'm guessing you two were on your way across the street to see me when you were almost plowed down. You may as well come in and have a cup of coffee while we chat."

"I would love a cup of coffee." Adeline stuck her arm through Mrs. McCall's and headed up the walkway. "I overslept and didn't have time to make a cup before rushing the boys out the door this morning."

Linc looked across the street at Ryan, shrugged and then turned, jogging to catch up with the ladies. Reaching them, he put a hand on Adeline's shoulder. "Could I have a moment to speak with you, alone, before we go inside?"

Adeline nodded. "Okay."

"Take your time, dearies. I'll make a fresh pot of coffee. The door will be unlocked. Come in when you're finished." Mrs. McCall ambled into the house, humming an unrecognizable tune under her breath.

"What is it? Is it something about the car that tried to run us over?" Adeline questioned as soon as the door closed behind the elder neighbor.

"No. I've already shared all the information I have on that." He took a deep breath and met her gaze. "I want to apologize. I'm sorry I snapped out orders earlier. In all honesty, you had more right to chase after the guy than I did. Ryan brought it to my attention that I can be a bit overbearing. For that, I'm sorry."

Shock registered in her eyes before she shuttered them.

"Thank you for apologizing. I'll admit, my feelings were hurt. Then Mrs. McCall came out and said she'd phoned the police, and once they arrived, it made sense for me to be here answering their questions." Adeline smiled.

It was the first genuine smile he'd seen on her face in a long time. The humiliation of needing to apologize melted away, and his heart felt lighter. "Promise me one thing. If I pull a stunt like that again, you'll call me out on it. Most of the time I don't realize I'm being a jerk. And friends should be able to tell each other when they're overstepping."

"Can we use that label—friends—for our relationship? Won't it complicate things?"

"I believe we can. The entire Protective Instincts brand was built on friendship. Ryan is my best friend. And his sister, Bridget, is like a sister to me. I would walk into any battle ground to fight with them and for them." He smiled. "Actually, I already have. When Bridget faced a serial killer, I was there. And you may recall, when Ryan needed backup on Christmas Eve in Wyoming, I was there, along with Bridget and her husband, Sawyer.

Seems to me, in our line of work, being friends makes us a stronger unit. Not weaker."

Tears glistened in her eyes, but she blinked them away. He was sure there was a lot more to Adeline's background story than she'd shared when he'd interviewed her. Maybe one day she'd feel comfortable sharing it with him.

"Okay. One last thing before we go inside. Prior to realizing that I had bulldozed my way into your private life, uninvited, and that I was making decisions regarding this situation and your and the twins' safety that weren't mine to make—"

"Get to the point already," Adeline ordered, a twinkle in her eyes.

"Ryan is across the street at your house with a new state-of-the-art security system that he's preparing to install."

"What!" She paced a few steps then swung around to glare at him. "I don't have money for that. Of all the things you've—" Adeline closed her eyes, took a deep breath and slowly released it.

"I'm sorry I made the decision to update the security system without asking you first. You don't have to pay any—"

She pinned him with a look his elementary school-teachers often used when he'd tried to talk his way out of trouble but, in reality, was only digging himself in deeper.

"I *will* pay for the equipment. You can pay for the labor since you're the one who ordered the services." She put her hand on the doorknob.

He cleared his throat. "Uh, Ryan needs the passcode for the existing security system so he can go inside and get to work."

"Fine. I'll call him." She pulled her phone out of her back pocket.

Linc didn't know what Ryan said on the other end of the phone, but by the time Adeline disconnected the call, a smile had reappeared on her face.

"We've kept Mrs. McCall waiting long enough." She tucked the phone away. "Oh, and…Linc. Thank you. Even though you should have cleared the new security system with me first, I know you meant well. Now let's catch this creep before he hurts my nephews."

He nodded and followed her indoors. Catching movement out of the corner of his eye, he saw Mrs. McCall step away from the window. But even her eavesdropping on a private conversation couldn't dampen his new sense of determination and purpose. Ryan had been right. Linc needed to communicate more and bark orders less.

Adeline called him *Linc* now. Not Lincoln or Mr. Jameson, which she had insisted on calling him until the night of the home invasion. Only friends called him Linc. He hoped this new comradery would give them a better working relationship. They just needed to capture the guy who'd broken into the house and find out what he was after, before Linc blew it again with his communication. Because no matter how well things had been smoothed over, it would be only a matter of time before he messed up and tried to run the operation again. After all, he was a former marine and the son of a four-star general. Being a leader and taking charge was as much a part of his DNA as his hair color.

FIVE

Adeline propped her elbows on the kitchen table and leaned forward. "Mrs. McCall, just because you saw Isaac sitting in a car with a woman doesn't mean he was having an affair. It could have been work-related. You know he owned a consulting firm. Maybe she was a client."

The older woman harrumphed. "That's what *he* said when I confronted him about it."

"You confronted him about the woman?" Linc asked.

"You better believe it. I love that little family." Her voice broke, and she dabbed at the tears that leaked out of the corners of her eyes. "I still can't believe Vanessa and Isaac are gone."

Adeline patted Mrs. McCall's hand. "I know. Me neither."

"And those precious boys. They need security and stability, now more than ever. You know that, right? Their needs must come before your wants." With her white hair in a bun and her blue eyes pinning Adeline to her chair, Mrs. McCall looked more like a prosecuting attorney than a friendly, albeit nosy, neighbor. "And don't you forget it."

Had Vanessa said something to Mrs. McCall to make her think Adeline wouldn't put the boys' needs first? If so, why had Vanessa named her guardian? She should have named their mother guardian. Adeline was sure she'd loved having her grandsons with her so she could spoil them. Besides, wasn't Adeline putting their needs first? If not, she would have put them on a plane to Florida the moment the funeral was over, or at least moved them into her condo.

Fighting the urge to squirm, she pressed her lips together, forced a smile, then glanced away. Linc was watching her. Did he also think she was a neglectful aunt?

Linc cleared his throat. "Back to the woman in the car. Do you remember anything about her?"

"No. She always parked down the street. Too far away for me to make out many details."

"You're sure it was a woman?" Adeline asked, still not believing Isaac would have an affair. He had been a loving husband and father. There was no way he'd risk losing Vanessa and the boys by having an extramarital relationship.

"Oh, yes. A few nights before Isaac and Vanessa's accident, I was having difficulty sleeping. I heard a car door slam just after midnight, so I got up to look outside." Mrs. McCall paused, as if waiting for them to agree with her.

"Naturally," Linc interjected. "And what did you see?"

"Isaac stood on the sidewalk in front of the Andersons' house—that's the Tudor-style, three doors down. He was in a heated discussion with the woman."

"Can you describe her? Height? Build?" Adeline asked.

The elder woman's brow wrinkled and she shook her head. "No. Unfortunately, I can't. She stayed in the shadows, but Isaac was under the streetlamp, so it was easy to see he was angry about something." Mrs. McCall started fiddling with the lace tablecloth. "Since this occurred just a few days after I confronted him about the woman, I wondered if maybe he was breaking it off with her and she was threatening to tell Vanessa about the affair." She shrugged and dabbed at the corners of her eyes. "I guess I'll never know."

"I'm sorry we've upset you. I appreciate you sharing these things with us. My sister was blessed to have you as a neighbor. Thank you for caring so much about my family."

Linc cleared his throat. "Before we go, I was wondering… What did you see last night?"

"I saw a man wearing a mask come out the front door. He just waltzed right out, closing it behind him before walking across the lawn to the sidewalk and heading up the street. His back was to me. Right after that, you turned onto the street and he hid behind a tree and watched as you went around the house. Then he jumped into a car that looked a lot like that one this morning and sped away." She turned to Linc and glared at him. "I will say, I didn't know if you were a good guy or a bad guy at that point, so I was frightened for Adeline and the boys." Turning to Adeline, she added, "I would have called to warn you, but I don't have your number."

Dutifully chastened, Adeline smiled. "As you can tell, Linc is a good guy, but I'll give you my number before we leave."

"Thank you, dear. I would appreciate that. Anyway, I called the police to report what I'd seen and was informed officers were en route."

"I noticed you looking out your window as the police drove by a few hours after that. Did you see anything unusual?" Linc queried.

"No. Nor did I spot anyone lurking around the other

times I glanced out during the night." She laughed. "At my age, it's not uncommon to wake up multiple times throughout the night. And after all the excitement earlier, I decided it wouldn't hurt to keep an eye on the neighborhood. I know the police cruiser drove by at least twice more."

Concern for the woman welled up inside Adeline, and she picked up the frail hand. "Mrs. McCall, I need you to promise me you'll be more careful. If Linc saw you looking out the window, the intruder could have as well. And if he thinks you can identify him, you'll be in danger."

"Thank you, dear, but I'm sure I'll be fine. Most people tend to overlook people my age. They write us off as being senile and don't feel threatened by our presence."

Linc withdrew his business card, flipped it over and wrote something on the back, then handed it to Mrs. McCall. "Adeline is right. We don't want you to put yourself in danger. If you see anything suspicious, anything at all, even if it's unrelated to this event, please call me or Adeline. I wrote mine and Adeline's private cell numbers on the back of the card."

"Okay, I guess we need to get going." Adeline pushed her chair away from the table. "I have your number. Vanessa gave it to me when I moved back to Denver, and I was watching the boys one evening. She said if I ran into trouble to call you. Now, I know why." She bent and hugged the woman, who'd been a fountain of information. "Thank you."

Linc and Adeline said their goodbyes and headed back across the street, jogging across the road this time.

"Well, that was a lot more information than I expected. Do you think your brother-in-law was having an affair?"

"I guess I can't rule it out, but I'd be shocked if it were

true. Isaac loved Vanessa. And even though it had always been his dream to follow in his father's footsteps and become a vice admiral in the navy, he gave all that up to open a consulting firm because he wanted to give Vanessa and the boys a settled life, not one where they were being moved around by the government."

"What kind of consulting firm did he start? And who's running it now?"

"I'm not sure. It's some kind of tech company, I think. His lawyer scheduled a meeting with me later this afternoon to go over the will and the business holdings."

"Would it be okay if I came along with you?"

Relief washed over her. She had been dreading the meeting. Adeline had never owned a business and, while she was sure Isaac had left the controlling interest in the business to the boys, someone would have to oversee the operations or—if decided—the sale of the business on their behalf.

"I would—" The sound of a drill swallowed her words.

"What did you say?" Linc yelled.

She paused at the foot of the porch steps and leaned in close, the woodsy scent of his aftershave wafting up her nose. "I would appreciate you going to the lawyer's office with me. It will be nice to have an extra set of ears keeping track of all the legal mumbo jumbo."

Linc nodded. "What time?"

"One o'clock. So, we'll be back before the boys."

He stepped back and held up his arm so they could both see the time—8:54. Almost two hours of the morning had slipped away, and they were still no closer to finding out what the intruder had been searching for.

"Looks like we have—" The vibration of her cell phone

halted her words. With both her bosses at her house, the only other people who would call would be her mother or the boys. She tugged the phone out of her back pocket, and the elementary school's number flashed on the screen. "I have to take this."

Adeline dashed up the steps and maneuvered her way around extension cords that snaked across the floor. When Ryan looked up with a smile, she used her hand to make a slashing sign across her neck, indicating he needed to cut the noise. Then she darted into the office, her finger sliding across the phone screen to answer the call at the same instant the house went silent.

Please, Lord, don't let Matthew or Josiah be in trouble or hurt.

Aware of Ryan standing in the doorway, Linc stood quietly behind Adeline and listened to her side of the conversation.

"No. The boys do not have an Uncle Theo… I didn't send anyone to check them out. Do not let them leave campus! I'm on my way!" She spun around and bumped into Linc, her eyes wide. "There's a man at the school trying to pick up the boys. I've got to go."

She brushed past him and Ryan, racing out of the office and down the hall toward the kitchen. Linc followed her, yelling over his shoulder for Ryan to stay at the house until they returned. Adeline snagged a key off a hook beside the refrigerator and yanked open the door leading to the garage. She pressed a button on the wall and the garage door opened, revealing his red sports car blocking her exit.

"Move your vehicle." She headed for the driver's side of her Jeep.

He caught her arm, halting her. "I'm coming with you. Let's just take mine. It'll be faster."

She looked like she might argue, but then she held out her hand. "Give me the keys."

"What?"

"I know the way. I'm driving. Your vehicle or mine. Doesn't matter." Determination shone in her eyes.

No one, other than himself, had ever driven his car. But this wasn't the time to argue a point. He pressed his lips together and dropped the keys into her open palm. For the second time that morning, he would be a passenger and not the one in the driver's seat. Not a place he was used to being, but maybe it was time he learned to relinquish control. At least a little.

He slid into the passenger seat as Adeline started the vehicle and clicked his seat belt into place as she backed onto the road. "I know we need to get there in a hurry, but we also need to arrive in one piece."

"Someone is trying to kidnap the boys."

"And the school is doing everything they're supposed to do. They called you to verify. And they won't let him have them since you told them you're the only one allowed to check them out."

She approached a stop sign, completed a rolling stop and made a sharp left turn. "I hope not. But I'd also like to get there before he leaves so we can find out who he is and what he's after."

The vehicle accelerated, and he reached out and placed a hand on the dashboard. "How far away is the school?"

"Ten minutes. Or less."

They rode in silence for the remainder of the trip. When they arrived at the school, the principal, Mr. Overton, greeted them, along with a uniformed school resource officer.

"I'm Adeline Scott, the boys' aunt and legal guardian." She displayed her driver's license for identification. "And this is my boss Lincoln Jameson."

Linc handed each of the men his business card.

Mr. Overton escorted them into his office. "Ms. Scott, you didn't have to rush to the school. The boys are fine. We would never let a student leave campus with someone not listed in their files as having authority to check them out. That's why the secretary called you."

"I appreciate that. Is the man claiming to be the boys' *Uncle Theo* still here?"

"No, ma'am." The SRO pulled a small notebook out of his front pocket. "When the secretary phoned you, the man ran out of the office. I was in a classroom when Mr. Overton alerted me to the situation. I ran to the parking lot. The man took off in a black sports car. I got the license plate number."

"May I see that, please?" Linc leaned over and looked at the number. "As I suspected. That's the same vehicle that tried to run over Ms. Scott this morning. The tag's stolen."

He turned to the principal. "Could we view the video footage you have of the man?"

"No. That's not possible." Mr. Overton shook his head. "We're not in the habit of allowing parents—or guardians— to view our school security tapes. I'd have to get board approval."

"These are highly unusual circumstances," Adeline said softly. She turned her full attention to Mr. Overton. "The boys lost their parents a week ago. Then last night someone broke into their home and, as of this morning, the boys and I have been targeted. We need to figure out who's behind the attacks before it's too late. Going to the board would take too long."

"I understand, but my hands are tied."

"Have you reported all the incidences to the police?" the SRO asked.

"Yes. Everything except this one. There was no time before rushing here," Addie explained.

Linc quickly sent a text to Ryan.

Call police. Report that someone tried to take the boys from school.

"Actually, my business partner is reporting the attempted kidnapping as we speak."

The SRO smiled at Linc and turned to Mr. Overton. "Since this is an established, ongoing investigation, and considering Ms. Scott's and Mr. Jameson's line of work, I believe we'd be within our rights to let them view a photo of the man who attempted to check out the boys. Don't you?"

"I'm not sure."

"Of course, it's your choice, Mr. Overton. This can be a simple process where you rewind the footage and take a screenshot photo of the man for us to view—and then we're out of your way—or it can be an all-day ordeal. We'll have the police come here to take our complaint, which I'm sure would require them also to take statements from everyone who interacted with the man." Linc pressed the phone button on his cell. "I can guarantee you, with a few phone calls—to a judge and a couple of the school board members our company has done work for—I will have the permissions I need to view the security footage before the end of the day."

"Oh, all right. I don't guess it can hurt." Mr. Overton plopped into his desk chair and pulled up the security footage on his computer. "No peeking until I have the man on the screen. I don't want any students' rights violated."

Adeline leaned close and whispered in Linc's ear, "Thank you." Then she turned to the SRO. "I'd like to check my nephews out of school. Since there's already been a kidnapping attempt on campus, would you mind going to their classrooms and escorting them to the office? I know that's asking a lot, but…"

"It's fine. You're concerned for their safety, and rightfully so. I'm happy to be of assistance." The officer smiled at Adeline and exited the room.

The printer on the cabinet behind the principal's desk sprang to life, spitting out a grainy photo of a man. Mr. Overton handed the printed sheet to Linc. "I thought you might want a copy to take with you, but I'm not sure how much it will help in identifying the man." He turned his computer monitor around so they could get a better view. "As you can see, he went to great lengths to hide his identity."

The man who had identified himself as the boys' "Uncle Theo" was well above six feet tall and broad-shouldered, fitting the description Adeline had given of the man who'd broken in the night before. He wore a baseball cap pulled low, dark sunglasses and an oversize trench-style raincoat. No more recognizable now than he had been last night.

"Thank you, for allowing us to view this." Adeline bit her lip in a move Linc had witnessed several times during the days leading up to the funeral. It seemed to be her way of fighting back tears.

Linc wished he could take away her pain from losing her sister and brother-in-law, and prevent her from experiencing more pain at the threat of losing her nephews. But there was nothing he could do. Except catch the person responsible. And that was something he fully intended to do, even if it meant putting other cases on hold. Family first. And Adeline was part of the Protective Instincts' family.

Yeah, right. Like that's the only reason you care about her pain.

Pushing the thought away, he held out his hand to the principal. "Yes, thank you. I appreciate you bending the rules to let us get a look at the man. I'm sure the police will want a copy of the security video footage."

Mr. Overton stood. "I wasn't trying to be difficult. Educators constantly face scrutiny from the public, so we have to be diligent about doing things by the book." He turned to Adeline. "I really am sorry for all that your family is going through. I hope you find the man who attempted to check out the boys."

She offered a forced smile. "I appreciate your staff being on top of the situation. Also, I hope you understand, but I'll keep the boys home until we catch this man."

"Of course. We can temporarily move them to remote learning. Leave your email address with my secretary, and I'll have her send instructions on accessing the lessons."

There was a light rap on the door and the SRO stuck his head inside. "I wanted to let you know the boys are ready to go."

Linc smiled at the sound of Matthew and Josiah talking in hushed tones in the hall. Matthew had assumed his big-brother role and was telling Josiah to follow his lead and that no matter how much trouble they were in, it would be okay.

Lincoln wished he could be as confident as Matthew that everything would be okay. Unfortunately, Linc had had too many experiences where things didn't always turn out the way one expected. *Lord, please, don't let me fail in this situation.*

SIX

A few minutes later, both boys sat fastened into the back seat of Linc's red sports car.

"I bet it can go fast," Josiah exclaimed.

"Of course, it can. It's like a race car," Matthew said.

Closing the rear door on their excited chatter, Adeline faced Linc. "In my rush to reach them, I didn't even think to get their booster seats out of my vehicle." Additional proof she wasn't qualified to be their guardian.

"In Colorado it's legal for children eight years old and above to be out of booster seats."

"Vanessa wanted them to be a little taller before they transitioned away from the boosters, and I wanted to honor her wishes." She shrugged. "At least until they really start to complain."

A smile split his handsome face. "And that's why you're going to be a great mom for these boys."

What was he talking about? Hadn't he been paying attention the past few days?

"Keys, please." Linc held out his hand. "Since it's *my* car and I now know the way, I'll drive this time."

She dropped the keys onto his palm then reached to open her door. He touched her arm and halted her. Adeline turned and arched an eyebrow. He jerked his head toward the front of the car, and she followed him, keeping the boys in sight at all times.

"What is it?" she asked in hushed tones.

"Do you think it's a good idea to take the boys back to the house while there's so much going on?"

"What do you mean?"

"It'll take Ryan a few more hours to finish the installation of the new security system, and the repairman will arrive soon to repair the boys' bedroom door and replace the glass in the back door. Aren't you concerned the boys will be more frightened if they learn the full extent of all that's going on?"

Adeline hadn't even considered what the boys would think if they saw the status of the house. Reason number one hundred sixty-three that no matter what anyone else thought, she would not be the best guardian for them. She wasn't used to thinking about what might or might not be ideal for eight-year-olds.

"You're probably right. The reason for us staying in their home instead of mine was to minimize the disruptions in their life and give them a sense of security." Her brow furrowed. "But what do you have in mind? We can't just drive around aimlessly. Not in your flashy red sports car that Mrs. McCall said the intruder saw last night."

"You make a valid point. However, when I was racing out the door to reach you, I was more concerned with speed than I was with discretion." He met her gaze. "After a quick stop at my house to change vehicles, I think we should take the boys to the zoo."

"The zoo?" Had her boss lost his edge? Were the boys making him soft? She couldn't imagine him ever suggesting taking a client they were guarding to the zoo. "Is it wise to hang out in such a public place? I would never forgive myself if anything happened to my nephews."

"Don't you know, it's easier to hide in a crowd? Taking the boys some place where there are other people their size around will make them blend in better. Besides, these boys have two of the best bodyguards in the business protecting them. Trust me. I wouldn't do anything that I thought would put either you or the twins in danger."

"I didn't mean to imply that you would. I'm sorry." She sighed. "Let's go get your nondescript black SUV. Once we're sure we haven't been followed, we'll decide about the zoo."

"Sounds like a plan."

"Not a word about the zoo, until then. Okay?"

"Deal." He guided her back to the passenger side, opened her car door, then jogged around the front of the vehicle, and slid into the driver's seat.

"Why'd you check us out of school, Aunt Addie?" Josiah asked.

"Oh, I just decided I'd like to spend the day with you." Addie turned to smile at the boys.

"Where are we going?" Josiah probed.

"On an adventure," Adeline replied.

"You said we've missed several days of school already, and if we miss many more, it will be harder to catch up on all our work." Matthew threw her words back at her almost verbatim.

She looked at Linc for support, and he just smiled and pulled out of the parking lot, headed east. Turning back to Matthew and Josiah, she shrugged. "What can I say? Sometimes adults change their minds."

The boys stared at her a few seconds then turned to each other and mimicked her shrug. "Okay, Aunt Addie," they said in unison.

Facing forward, Adeline puffed out a breath and settled into her seat. Through the drive, she periodically glanced in the rearview mirror to check for anyone tailing them.

"Did someone else die?" Matthew asked softly, fifteen minutes into the drive.

She gasped and turned in her seat to face the boys. "No. Oh, no. It's nothing like that at all."

"You promise?" Josiah looked up at her with pleading eyes. Matthew reached across and patted his brother's hand.

"I promise." Her arms ached to wrap the boys in a big hug. She'd never dreamed they would think someone else had died. Would she ever learn how to handle delicate situations like this? She'd at least like to get through the next six weeks without adding to their trauma. It was bad enough that they'd lost their parents, they didn't need her making things worse by mishandling every situation that arose. "We're going to Linc's house to swap vehicles. Then we're going to the zoo, where you can eat junk food and ride a train."

"Oh, boy! The zoo!" Josiah exclaimed. He listed all the animals he wanted to see.

Matthew leaned back against his seat, crossed his arms over his little chest and stared at her, his eyes boring into her as if he were trying to get inside her head to figure out what she was thinking. "Why today? Mom wouldn't like this. School should come first. We could have gone to the zoo on Saturday."

"True, but…"

"It will be less crowded today," Linc interjected, never

taking his eyes off the road. "Consider it a field trip. Maybe your teacher will let you do a report for extra credit. You can use my phone to take a video to share with your class."

"Come on, Matthew. Don't be a spoilsport. Remember the time Dad checked us out of school and took us to the movies? He said we were making memories." Josiah smiled. "It's a great day to make more memories."

"I guess." Matthew sighed and looked out the window.

Linc leaned over and whispered, "I thought you were going to wait to tell them about the zoo."

She shrugged, not taking her eyes off the boys as Josiah drew Matthew into a conversation about which animals they would see. "You heard him. I couldn't let him think something bad had happened again."

Convinced Josiah would keep Matthew's mind off negative thoughts, Adeline settled into her seat and cast a quick glance in her boss's direction. "Just make sure we aren't followed, so we can give the boys a nice day."

"Of course." He activated his blinker and turned into a gated community.

Adeline watched as the gate closed behind them, relief washing over her for the first time since they'd picked the boys up from school. At least, if someone had been tailing them, they wouldn't be able to follow them into the neighborhood and see them swap vehicles.

Three hours later, Linc watched as the boys and Adeline fed the giraffes. It had taken a bit of coaxing, but Matthew had relaxed enough to have fun with his brother and aunt, though he was still mildly cool to Lincoln. Linc didn't take it personally since the boy had never spent time around him before.

His cell phone vibrated. Ryan's number flash on the screen. Getting Adeline's attention, he held up his phone and motioned to her he was going to move beside the snack stand. She nodded and turned back to the boys. Never taking his eyes off the trio, he slid his finger across the phone screen and lifted it to his ear. "Hi, Ryan."

"I wanted to let you know I finished installing the security system and the repairman just left. The back door looks as good as new, and the boys' bedroom door frame has been repaired."

"Thanks, buddy." Linc smiled as Addie took selfies of her and the boys with a momma giraffe and her calf. "I hate to ask, but do you mind hanging around until we get back? I'd really like someone to be there if the intruder comes back."

"Sure. No problem."

"Great. I want to let the boys pick out a toy from the gift shop, and then we'll head that way." A father and child walked up, and he stepped aside so they could read the menu posted on the side of the snack stand.

"You know, if you're not careful, you'll get too attached to those kids."

"Not a chance. I just feel bad for all they've been through. That's all."

Ryan laughed. "Sure, tell yourself that, but remember, I speak from experience."

Linc was happy his friend had found love and was now a father to a sweet seven-year-old, but he refused to let Ryan goad a reaction out of him. His situation was different for many reasons. For one, even if he wasn't determined to remain a bachelor, he had no intention of crossing the line and dating an employee, and for another,

Adeline had told him on the phone last night when she'd asked for an extended leave that she was going to give up her guardianship of the boys once the school year was over. "Yes, but the kids are going to live wi—"

"Ahem."

He spun around to find three sets of eyes staring at him. How had they sneaked up on him? He'd only looked away for a moment. "Ryan, I've gotta go. We'll be back at the house soon." Disconnecting the call, he slipped the phone into his pocket. "All finished feeding the giraffes?"

"Yes. And it seems like we finished just in time," Adeline said through gritted teeth.

"What kids were you talking about, Mr. Jameson?" Josiah asked.

"Um. It was nothing important. I was—"

"Us. Josiah. He was talking about us." Matthew glared at Adeline. "You promised we'd stay in our house. We don't want to move to yours!"

Adeline dropped to her knees in front of the twins. "I know, sweetie. And I promise I won't move you to my condo."

"I can vouch for that. She told me the same thing last…" Adeline pushed to her feet and turned on him. He bit off the remaining words.

I've got this, she mouthed.

He'd put his foot in his mouth this time. Adeline had told him she was still working out the logistics. He should have known the boys didn't have any idea what their aunt was up to. Linc wasn't even sure their aunt knew what she was doing. He suspected Adeline would regret turning her back on her sister's kids. Oh, well, it wasn't any of his business. All he could do at this point was keep the boys safe and pray Adeline made the right choice for all of them. "Okay, we've seen all the animals. I thought we'd make a quick stop by the gift shop so you guys could get a souvenir of our adventure."

"Oh, boy! I want a rhinoceros. No, an elephant. Or a zebra." Josiah grabbed Adeline's hand and started pulling her toward the exit where the gift shop was located. "Come on, Matthew. Don't you want a toy?"

Matthew looked Linc up and down then huffed and turned to follow his brother and aunt. "I'm coming," he yelled.

One thing was for certain, Ryan was way off base if he thought Lincoln was in danger of getting too attached to the boys and vice versa. Matthew had an imaginary brick wall built around himself, and he would surely convince Josiah to distance himself from Linc, too, once they had a moment alone.

That was fine by him. He didn't need to entangle himself in his employee's life any more than necessary. His only mission was to keep her and her charges safe from harm while helping her get answers to her sister's murder. He may have thought Adeline wasn't thinking clearly when she'd first mentioned the idea that the car accident that had claimed the lives of her sister and brother-in-law hadn't been an accident, and someone had killed them. But he knew better, now. He also knew the only way to convince the police would be if they found solid evidence. Until then, it would be up to him to keep Adeline and the boys safe.

"Boys, hurry and pick out a toy. It's time to go." Adeline picked up a stuffed penguin and put it back on the shelf it had fallen from. She was convinced Matthew and Josiah had touched every toy in the gift shop. Her stomach growled, and she laughed to mask the sound. The miles they'd walked at the zoo had burned off all the calories from the hotdogs and pretzels they'd eaten when they'd first arrived. "I don't know about you guys, but I'm getting hungry. The sooner we pay for our purchases, the sooner we can get home and I can make spaghetti and meatballs."

"Okay, Aunt Addie. We're ready." Matthew grabbed Josiah's hand and guided him toward the register where Linc stood watching them.

Both boys had settled on stuffed animals. Josiah had selected a fox, and Matthew had chosen a hedgehog. She smiled as the cashier rang up their purchases. The toys fit each boy's personality. Josiah was quiet and sly like a fox while Matthew put up a protective boundary around himself like the hedgehog.

The cashier rattled off the total, and Adeline reached into her back pocket for her wallet.

"This is on me." Linc slipped his credit card into the card reader.

"I can't let you do that." Her boss had insisted on paying their admittance to the zoo and buying their lunch. He'd said it was a business expense since he was protecting an employee. Adeline hadn't argued with him, but this was too much.

"Too late." He smiled and accepted the receipt from the cashier. Then he turned to Adeline. "I'll tell you what. I heard you talking about making spaghetti. You feed me dinner, and we'll call it even."

Matthew put his hand on his hip and huffed. "Aren't you ever going home?"

Lincoln laughed. "Eventually. But you wouldn't send a single man home to eat a frozen pizza, would you?" He crossed his hands over his chest as if the idea wounded him.

"Of course not. Come on, Mr. Jameson. Let's go home." Josiah reached up and slipped his small hand into Linc's larger one.

"It's *our* home, Josiah. Not his." Matthew shrugged. "But I guess it's okay for him to eat dinner with us. Since he brought us to the zoo and got us these toys."

Adeline's boss placed a hand on Matthew's shoulder and smiled at her, a strange expression on his face. She was in trouble. If they didn't capture the person after them soon, the boys and Linc would become too attached to each other.

"Thank you, boys. Okay, Addie, let's go." Linc guided the boys to the exit.

Her cell phone rang. The words Unknown Caller ID flashed on the screen. She motioned for Linc to come closer and slid a finger across the screen. "Hello?"

"Looks like the boys have had fun at the zoo today, but don't make the mistake of thinking they're safe. Because they aren't," a digitally altered voice said in her ear. She tilted her head and pulled the phone away just enough for Linc to hear. "Oh, and don't think a new security system will stop me from getting back into the house. Even your bosses at Protective Instincts aren't smart enough to one-up me. They'll let their guard down, and when they do, I'll take care of you *and* get what I'm after." The line went dead.

She met Linc's gaze. "How does he know so much about us?"

"I don't know." Linc shook his head. "But he's wrong about two things. He won't breach the security system, and he won't harm you. Or the boys. Ryan and I will make sure of that."

Gratitude swelled in her heart at the thought of having people in her life who had her back for a change. But the realization that the person after them continued to stay a step ahead squashed her joy. It didn't matter how many people would help protect her and the boys if they couldn't figure out who was after them, and why.

"Okay, so the first thing we need to do is get the boys home, where that new unbreachable security system can protect them." Adeline had never been someone who wanted to hide, preferring to face trouble head-on. But this time, she had to think of the twins. She would do whatever it took to keep them safe. Even if that meant staying inside her sister's house with a security system and guards, and letting someone else take the lead on the case.

"Agreed. How do you want to do this?" Linc searched her face. "We can each tote a boy and run. Or I can leave you here while I go get the vehicle and pick you all up."

"What's going on?" Josiah asked.

"Nothing for you to worry about." She wrapped her arm around his shoulder and hugged him close, her heart racing as she struggled to decide between Linc's two options. Needing to know both boys were safe, she reached behind with her free hand to pull Matthew closer. Nothing but air. Adeline looked over her shoulder. He wasn't there. "Matthew! Where's Matthew?" She turned back to Linc and Josiah.

"He went over there to look at the lion." Josiah pointed at a large Lego sculpture of a lion across the store, near the double doors that led to the animal enclosure side of the zoo.

Adeline watched as a large man in a hoodie and sunglasses picked up Matthew, slung him over his shoulders and ran into the zoo area. "No!" She darted around a mother and her young daughter and raced toward the person carrying her nephew. "Stop that man!" she yelled at no one in particular, desperate for someone to step in and prevent the abduction. Vaguely aware of onlookers stopping to stare, she kept her eyes focused on her target.

Matthew kicked at his abductor's chest and beat on his back with his tiny fist. "Put me down! Aunt Addie, help!"

"Security! That stranger is abducting my child!"

The abductor turned sharply to the right and headed for the entrance. If he made it to his vehicle before she could catch him... Her chest tightened. *Lord, please, let someone stop him.*

Linc tugged on her shoulder, slowing her slightly, and shoved Josiah into her arms. "Here. Take him. I'll get Matthew." He raced past her, a uniformed guard on his heels.

Josiah buried his face into her neck. "The bad guy took Matthew."

"I know, honey, but Linc will save him." Adeline prayed she spoke the truth. If they didn't stop the man from leaving with Matthew, she'd never be able to face Josiah again. And she'd never be able to forgive herself.

Four additional guards showed up on the scene. Two from inside the zoo and two from the parking area. The abductor must have seen them closing in, too. He darted his head left and right. Linc closed in on him and stretched his hand out to grasp Matthew. The man half turned and shoved Matthew toward Linc. Adeline hugged Josiah close as Linc wrapped his arms around Matthew and stumbled into the guard behind him. The abductor rammed his way past the people trying to enter the zoo, pushing them into the guards approaching him. The car that had tried to run them over that morning sat at the curb. The abductor hopped inside and zoomed off. He had gotten away. Again.

Still holding Josiah close, Adeline jogged to meet Linc and Matthew. She held out her free arm and her normally tough-acting nephew dove into her arms. Her knees buckled and Linc wrapped his powerful arms around her. Her boss may not have intended to be part of the group hug, but once again, she was thankful for his support. This time literally.

"Folks, let me take you to the security office where there aren't so many spectators." A guard motioned to a door behind the ticket booth that bore the nameplate Security.

"I'll give you and the boys a few minutes, and then I'll come inside," Linc said in her ear.

The moment the door was closed and the three of them were alone, she put the boys down on the floor and knelt to face them. Her nephews weren't babies. They were almost nine years old, and there was no way she could continue to act like nothing was wrong. The twins were too smart to fall for an act. "I'm pretty sure that was the guy who broke into the house last night. The phone call was to let me know he knew we were here."

"What does he want from us?" Matthew asked.

"I don't know, but whatever it is, he won't stop until he finds it. I'm afraid if he gets another chance, he'll harm us." She took a deep breath and pushed it out slowly. "Which is why I've arranged for you to do your schoolwork online. You'll be at home where my bosses and I can keep you safe and you won't be behind when you return to school."

Adeline searched her nephews' faces. "This means Linc or my other boss, Ryan, will be with us at all times, helping guard you both, and the house. I need you to follow whatever instructions we give you. Do you understand?"

"Yes, Aunt Addie," the twins said in unison.

She hated the fear she saw in Josiah's eyes, but it was the fear in Matthew's eyes that was almost her undoing. Hanging back and not putting on his normal brave front was to be expected after his near abduction, but his loss of innocence weighed heavily on her chest. Her heart broke that she hadn't been able to shield him and Josiah from the harsh reality of the situation they'd found themselves in. She could do nothing other than pray at this point.

Lord, I know You've not answered most of my prayers through the years and I started doubting You, but please don't let anything happen to the boys. Don't let me fail at the one task Vanessa trusted me with the most. Protecting her sons.

SEVEN

"Now, it seems, the person who's been threatening my employee and her nephews has found us here," Linc said, after giving the security guard his business card and an abridged version of the situation.

"Do you believe the person is waiting for you outside?" the guard asked.

Linc looked through the small window in the door at Addie kneeling on the floor, hugging both boys. "It's a strong possibility."

"Where are you parked?"

"In the parking garage."

The security guard pulled out his walkie-talkie. "Okay, let me radio for assistance, and we'll escort you to your vehicle."

Linc nodded. "Thank you. I'll contact the police to let them know of the most recent attack. They'll probably want to see the security footage from this afternoon. Maybe there will be something on the video to help us identify the guy."

"No problem. We'll cooperate fully with the police."

Linc opened the door and went inside, where Adeline and the boys waited. "Everything okay here?"

Adeline pushed to her feet and hugged the boys close to her sides. "Yes. I filled in the boys about what's happening. And they're going to be excellent listeners as we make our way to your vehicle. Right, guys?"

Two small heads bobbed up and down, somber expressions on both boys' faces.

Linc hated that the seriousness of the situation had erased the smiles he'd seen earlier as they'd toured the zoo, but he hoped they would do as their aunt had instructed and follow directions so there wouldn't be a repeat of the near abduction. Though he couldn't blame Matthew for wanting to get a closer look at that Lego sculpture. Linc was more upset with himself for having taken his eyes off Matthew long enough for the man to grab him.

"Good. The security supervisor is arranging an escort to our vehicle."

There was a rap on the door and the security supervisor poked his head inside. "Okay, folks, we're ready to go." He swung the door wide, revealing two golf carts. "You four will ride with me, and two guards will follow behind in the other cart."

They piled into the larger golf cart, Linc in the front, beside the security guard, and Adeline and the twins in the back seat. Linc's thoughts returned to the near abduction. How had the guy found them at the zoo? Linc was sure the black sports car hadn't followed them earlier. He prayed the abductor didn't know what kind of vehicle they were driving and he could get his employee and her charges safely home.

"That's our vehicle." He pointed to his SUV and the security officer pulled to a stop behind it. "Thank you for your help."

The drive back to the twins' home was much quieter than the drive to the zoo had been. The boys rode in silence. Linc glimpsed them in the rearview mirror randomly shaking their heads or shrugging their shoulders. He wondered if they were communicating via some twin secret code or something, but thought it best not to say anything. If they wanted to talk about what had happened, they'd say something to their aunt.

They were only a few minutes from the house, and there had been no sign of the sports car. Still, he'd like to get his passengers out of his vehicle and indoors without prying eyes.

He leaned closer to Adeline. "Will I be able to park in the garage?"

She turned to him, taking her eyes off the side mirror for the first time since they'd left the parking garage. "Um. Sure. I'll need to move my vehicle out first, but that won't be a problem."

When he'd gone into the garage last night to get lumber to board up the back door, two vehicles had been parked inside. Adeline's Jeep and a minivan that had most likely belonged to Vanessa. "Why don't I have someone from the office come get the van? We can store it in the basement garage at Protective Instincts until you decide what to do with it."

"What? No." She shook her head. "I'd rather leave the van where it is. At least until we've settled the estate."

"Okay, but why not move the van to the curb in front of the house and leave your Jeep in the garage. That way, if the need arises, both of our vehicles are in a position where we can load up without prying eyes. Then no one will know who is or isn't inside when we leave."

"I can always drive Vanessa's van if necessary. We'll just leave it where it is."

"Sure. It's your call." Last night while clearing the house, Linc noticed Adeline's things were in the guest bedroom. The master bedroom had appeared to be untouched since the accident—discarded clothes draped across the neatly made bed and a pair of men's shoes on the floor. It seemed Adeline was having a much harder time with her sister's death than she'd let on.

Of course, no one understood the loss of a sibling more than he did, having lost his only sister, Jessica, seven years ago when an ex-boyfriend had brutally murdered her. Linc's mother had wanted to keep all of Jessica's items untouched, and his parents had paid the rent for Jessica's apartment for six months because it had been hard for them to let it go. It hadn't been until Linc and Ryan, who had been engaged to Jessica at the time of her murder, had convinced his parents to attend grief counseling that they'd had a breakthrough and been able to let go enough to box up Jessica's belongings.

Maybe when all this was over, he could encourage Adeline to do the same. Attending grief counseling had been the only thing to keep Linc from falling into a dark abyss he couldn't climb out of. He tapped his fingers on the steering wheel. "Is there a key to your Jeep at the house?"

"Yes. Why?"

"Would you mind if Ryan moved it? That way we don't have to sit in the drive waiting for it to be moved, making ourselves targets."

"Oh. Of course." She pulled out her phone and sent a text message. Soon after, her phone dinged in response. "Okay. Done."

Adeline turned to look into the back seat, and Linc glanced in the rearview mirror. Both boys were looking out their side windows, not saying a word, yet they held hands as if they were afraid to let go of each other.

"We're almost home," Adeline said cheerfully. "Are you guys ready for my famous spaghetti and meatballs?"

Two identical shrugs were the only response.

Turning back around, she settled into her seat with a sigh. "My sister left me one job, and I've failed," she whispered so only Linc could hear.

Before he could second-guess his actions, Linc reached across and squeezed her hand. "No, you haven't. We'll keep them safe. And we'll capture the person behind the attacks."

We'll keep them safe. She knew he'd said the words to comfort her, but they'd reinforced her failure. One job. Protect the twins. *And help them through their grief.* Okay, two jobs. She'd failed at both. By not stopping the intruder the instant he'd entered their home, she had put them both in danger and allowed more fear and grief to be heaped upon their tiny shoulders.

Linc made a left turn onto the street where the boys lived, and the house came into view. Ryan had parked her Jeep in the driveway, far enough back that she could get Vanessa's van out if needed, and the garage door was open. Ryan hopped out of the Jeep and rounded the front as they turned onto the drive. He trailed them into the garage.

"Who's that man?" Matthew demanded, fear lacing his words.

"It's okay. He's one of the good guys. His name is Ryan. He's my other boss." Adeline smiled at her nephews as Linc turned off the engine. "He's been watching the place while we were at the zoo."

Josiah frowned. "Was he here so the bad guy couldn't come back in the house while we were gone?"

"The bad guy will not come into the house again. I promise." Now, why had she said that? She knew better than to make promises she had no control over. Only, there were things she could control. She could keep her weapon close *and* have it be out of reach of little hands. And she could stop being stubborn and gratefully accept the help her bosses were offering to ensure that the boys had the around-the-clock protection they needed.

"Mom said don't make promises you can't keep." Matthew gave her a pointed look as he hopped out of the vehicle.

"Ah, but your aunt isn't making empty promises," Linc interjected, coming around the front of the vehicle with Josiah beside him. "While we were gone, Ryan installed a new security system that will alert us if anyone tries to get into the house."

Ryan strode to the wall console beside the door that led to the mudroom then lowered the garage door. "And I also installed a doggy door and gave Gunther a brand-new collar."

"What'd you do that for?" Josiah asked.

"Safety. The collar acts as a remote that activates the doggy door to open. Otherwise, it is locked tight." Ryan opened the mudroom door. "Who wants to see how it works?"

"Me!" both boys yelled in unison and trailed after Ryan into the kitchen, shooting off one question after the other as they went.

"What happens if Gunther breaks the collar?"

"What if the bad guy comes in the backyard and takes the collar from Gunther?"

"What if the power goes out?"

Linc draped his arm around her shoulders and leaned close to her ear. "Okay, I have to admit that last question was a good one. Maybe we need to hear Ryan's answer?"

Adeline laughed. "Oh, but I don't need to hear his answer. I already know it."

"You do, huh? What happens if the power goes out?"

"There's a whole-house generator that kicks in when there's a power outage."

He chuckled. "I can hear the boys now. 'What if that goes out, *Aunt Addie*?'"

"Then we light candles, nail a board over the doggy door, and get Mr. Linc and Mr. Ryan to stand guard outside. How does that sound, *Mr. Linc*?" She looked up at him. Her breath caught in her throat, and her heart did a funny little dance in her chest.

Adeline was suddenly aware of how close Linc stood to her, his arm around her shoulders. When had she started thinking of him as Linc and not Lincoln? She had refused to use his nickname, or any of her coworkers' nicknames for that matter, believing that it blurred boundaries that were so important in the workplace. Realization dawned that she'd been referring to him as Linc most of the day, and that it would be impossible to think of him any other way going forward. At some point, he'd changed from boss to friend. Fine. She could keep boundaries in place. Being friendly with her boss didn't have to mean they were crossing any lines or that they would start hanging out after work. Once this situation was over, things would go back to the way they'd been before. After work hours, he'd have his life, and she'd have hers. They wouldn't have to cross paths unless it was business-related.

All she had to do was stop the person after her and the boys, and figure out what her brother-in-law had been involved in that had gotten him and her sister killed and left her nephews orphans. And she needed to do it sooner rather than later. If she could wrap up this situation and send Linc back to his own home, complications would be minimal. Then they could go back to business as usual.

Keep telling yourself that. Maybe, eventually, you'll even believe it's possible.

Adeline stepped away from Linc and his arm dropped to his side. An icy shiver replaced the warmth he'd felt as they'd stood close. Effectively putting him in his place. He should have known better than to try to have a moment of comradery with her the way he would with Ryan or Bridget, or honestly, any other member of his team.

Adeline had put up barriers since the moment she'd arrived in Denver. Some internal instinct told him it was a protective measure and not a character trait. The past ten hours had reinforced that notion, and he'd hoped they were becoming more than boss and employee. Not that he wanted them to be close in a "let's date" kind of way, but, rather, he wanted them to be friends who weren't always on guard with each other and could kid around occasionally. He'd never cross the boss-employee boundary romantically. Doing so would put the entire team at risk. People who let their hearts become too invested became careless and didn't think clearly, which was not something that needed to happen when you were protecting someone from a would-be killer.

Adeline headed for the door. "I think it's time we save Ryan from the twins. They're probably hammering him with questions."

A frown sprang to his lips but he plastered a smile in its place, praying she hadn't noticed. "Don't forget Ryan has a daughter and having spent time around her, I imagine she can spit out more questions in a minute than both boys combined."

An image of Ryan's precocious stepdaughter, Sophia, came to mind. She was the most inquisitive child Linc had ever met. Even after being kidnapped and held in a small cabin on Christmas Eve, the moment they'd rescued her, she'd started talking nonstop, asking questions about how they'd found her and wanting to know all the things that had occurred after the kidnapper had taken her. Yep, Ryan could handle anything the twins threw at him.

When they entered the house, the kitchen was empty, but they could hear the boys talking in the front room. Adeline headed down the hall and he trailed behind. They found Ryan showing the boys how the new security system worked.

"Will there be laser beams all over the house at night?" Josiah asked.

"Actually—"

"Oh, boy!" Matthew interjected, interrupting Ryan. "We can pretend to be cat burglars and crawl under the beams."

"Yeah!" both boys said in unison, jumping around and high-fiving.

"Wait." Josiah stopped and frowned. "We don't have a cat."

"So? That movie mom liked had a cat burglar, and he

stole jewelry." Matthew shrugged. "I guess if there's no cat, you can take other stuff. Like cookies."

Shouts of jubilation resumed. Adeline placed a hand on each tiny shoulder and bent to eye level. "Hold on a minute. First, there will be no cookie thieves in this house—"

"Aww, Aunt Addie."

"You're not fun."

"Second, there aren't any indoor laser sensors. If there were, you guys would surely set them off multiple times a night. Also…" She grinned. "Don't believe everything you see on television. In real life, laser beams are invisible, not red or blue."

"Really?"

Matthew looked at the two men, apparently seeking a more expert opinion than that of his aunt. "Is that true, Mr. Ryan?"

Although Linc had been around the child for most of the day, Matthew had bonded with Ryan, whom he'd known for less than ten minutes. The sting of rejection pierced Linc's pride.

Don't take it personally. Ryan showed him the security system, so it makes sense he'd know the answer.

Ryan crossed his arms and leaned against the wall. "I'm afraid so."

Both boys looked from one adult to the other, their frowns deepening as they locked eyes with Adeline. Her face impassive, she straightened. "Okay, guys, now that you've seen the new security system, I think it's time you feed Gunther then go upstairs and get cleaned up for dinner."

"Yes, Aunt Addie. Come on, Gunther." Matthew looped his arm around Josiah's neck, and they headed down the hall. "I'm glad there aren't any laser beams. Now it will be even easier to sneak cookies," he said in a child's attempt at a whisper.

Linc snickered, and Adeline nailed him with a stern expression. He shrugged and playfully rolled his eyes. "Kids."

At that, Ryan burst into laughter and, like a yawn setting off an involuntary chain reaction, Linc and Adeline joined in. They all gasped for breath and tried to regain composure. Adeline wiped tears from her eyes. He couldn't remember the last time he'd heard her laugh. While he knew their laughter was an overreaction to the stress of the day, it brought him a moment's joy to see the relaxed expression on her face.

Matthew and Josiah returned from feeding Gunther, looked at the adults and shook their heads. "Grown-ups," they muttered and raced up the stairs, sending the adults into another fit of laughter.

"Okay, folks… I think that's my cue…to go home and see my beautiful bride and sweet daughter," Ryan said as he regained composure. He turned to Linc. "Call me if you need me. Zane and Lucy will be here around nine thirty. They'll stay in their vehicle while watching the house tonight, so you both can get some sleep. They have instructions to notify both of us if they see anything suspicious."

"You're stationing bodyguards outside? Don't they have enough to do?" Adeline questioned. "Why make them work overtime? I don't want my coworkers—"

"No one's making them do anything. When the staff heard about the situation, they made a nightly rotation schedule and came to me with it." Ryan smiled. "They hope you guys can get a little sleep knowing someone else has the night shift covered."

"Like I told you, Protective Instincts is not just a business. We're a family. We take care of each other," Linc chimed in. "It would hurt your coworkers' feelings if we told them they couldn't donate their free time to help protect you and the boys."

He wished he understood why it was so difficult for her to accept help. He prayed she'd realize she didn't have to face things alone anymore. "Ryan, tell everyone thanks."

"Will do." Ryan turned and pulled Adeline into a friendly embrace. "I know this is stressful. You're doing a great job, and the boys will be fine. Just continue to love them and reassure them you're not going anywhere."

Adeline returned Ryan's embrace. "Thank you. I appreciate all you've done."

A pang of jealousy stabbed Linc's heart. Only a little while ago, she had bolted when Linc had casually placed his arm across her shoulders. Why was she returning Ryan's hug? He pushed the hurt aside. Adeline could hug whomever she wanted. Besides, Ryan was a stepfather. If anyone knew how hard it was to become an instant parent, it was him.

Linc hoped she would take comfort in the words his best friend offered. He was grateful for Ryan and his ability to read the situation and know Adeline needed encouraging. But, at the moment, he couldn't push past the overwhelming sense of rejection that Adeline accepted friendship from someone other than him. He sighed. This was no time to analyze those feelings. Plus, once this case was over and they had captured the person after Adeline and the boys, life would go back to normal and those feelings, whatever they were, would disappear. He hoped.

EIGHT

The boys will be fine. Just continue to love them and reassure them you're not going anywhere. Adeline's brain replayed Ryan's parting words as she loaded the dishwasher after dinner. She knew her boss meant for his words to be reassuring, but they weren't. Because, while she wasn't going anywhere, the boys were. Sooner than she intended, if things got worse and she couldn't ensure their safety.

Adeline never realized her bosses were the hugging types until today. She had awkwardly patted Ryan's shoulder and stepped out of the embrace as quickly as she could. Then she'd turned and seen the frown on Linc's face. He'd disapproved of her hugging Ryan, a married man. So much for the wall she'd built to guard herself from getting too close to her colleagues. She doubted she'd ever be able to rebuild it as solidly as she had before. Once this ordeal was over, she would need to decide if she could stick around or if she should find a new job. But there was no use worrying about that now. She had to compartmentalize her problems and deal with one issue at a time.

The sounds of Linc and the boys playing in the backyard drew her attention out the kitchen window. As much as she hated to need the help of others, she was thankful Ryan had installed the new security system complete with motion sensor cameras around the property line. If it wasn't for that added security, she never would have felt comfortable letting the boys play outside. Matthew was on the patio with Gunther, trying to teach the dog to sit on command, while Linc and Josiah tossed a football back and forth. The sun sank low on the horizon and dusk settled over the yard. What time was it? She looked at the clock on the stove—7:13. Time for the boys to start their nighttime routine before bed. Adeline placed the last dish into the dishwasher, added detergent and started the machine.

Wiping her hands on a towel, she crossed to the door, opened it, and stuck her head outside. "Time to get ready for bed boys."

"Ah, Aunt Addie, five more minutes."

"Gunther hasn't mastered rolling over yet."

"Sorry, guys, you need to brush your teeth, wash up and tidy your room before bed if you expect a bedtime story tonight." Addie stood her ground. The only normalcy she'd been able to hang on to had been their nightly bedtime routine.

Vanessa had told her, the first time she'd babysat after returning to Denver, the bedtime routine was her favorite part of the day. She and Isaac would put the boys to bed and take turns telling them a bedtime story. Her sister had said she hoped these were the memories her sons carried with them for the rest of their lives. Vanessa had even dreamed of the boys carrying on the tradition with their own families one day. Of course, Adeline couldn't imagine why any mother of seven-year-olds would plan for the time she became a grandmother, but if the tradition of a bedtime story was important to Vanessa, then it was important to Adeline. She knew, as Vanessa had, the boys would outgrow being tucked in with a bedtime story in a couple of years.

The boys tromped into the kitchen.

"Okay, get cleaned up and in your PJs. I'll be upstairs soon to tuck you in and tell you a bedtime story."

"Do you have to tuck us in and tell us a story?" Matthew grumbled. "I'm too big to be treated like a baby."

"You didn't mind it last week when Dad was telling us a story," Josiah interjected.

"Last week, Dad was the man of the house. This week, I am." Matthew's voice cracked, and he ran out of the room.

"I want Mom and Dad to come home," Josiah cried and threw his arms around Addie's waist.

"I know, sweetie. I'm sorry." She rubbed the back of his shoulders and held him close for several minutes. "Run on upstairs. I'll be right behind you. If Matthew doesn't want to listen to the story, he doesn't have to. But that doesn't mean you can't."

Josiah wiped the tears from his eyes, nodded, then shuffled out of the room.

"You're great with them." Linc crossed to the sink and washed his hands.

What should someone say when they knew the compliment being given wasn't true? *Never argue over a compliment.* Her mother's voice echoed in her mind. *Graciously accept them. Compliments are meant to make you feel appreciated and seen. Even if you don't agree with the thought, simply say 'Thank you' and be appreciative someone took the time to tell you something they thought you'd like to hear.*

"Thank you." Adeline hoped her response hadn't sounded as flat to Linc's ears as it had hers. She really needed to work on her people skills. Why was she so bad at being friendly and outgoing? Addie sighed softly. All the more reason to send the boys to live with her parents. They didn't need to turn out like her.

Linc gave her a tight-lipped smile, snagged the dishcloth from the counter, crossed to the table and started dusting crumbs into the palm of his hand.

She reached for the cloth, but he pulled it out of her grasp.

"I've got this." He looked toward the hall. "Go do the bedtime thing with the boys. I'll take the trash out then make sure everything is locked up tight."

Adeline opened her mouth but quickly closed it. *Don't argue. He's here and doesn't mind helping.* Besides, he was right. The boys were waiting. And the sooner she settled them into bed, the sooner she could dig into Isaac's files to find what the intruder had been after. "Okay, I'll meet you in Isaac's office in twenty minutes."

Her boss nodded and continued with his chores, softly whistling a tune she didn't recognize.

Fifteen minutes later, after they'd brushed their teeth, picked up and put away the toys scattered around their room, and changed into pajamas, the boys were settled into their twin beds. Matthew, having refused to be *tucked in*, lay in his bed, reading a library book from school, while Josiah waited for Adeline to read him a bedtime story.

"What story would you like me to read?" Adeline perused the boys' bookshelves. "Do you want one about dinosaurs? Or maybe one about—"

"I want to hear the story of *The Pirate and the Princess.*"

She ran her finger along the book spines. "I don't see a book about a pirate or a princess."

"It's not a book," Matthew said without looking up from his own book. "It's a story Dad made up. He preferred making up his own over reading us *boring stories.*"

"I imagine your father was an excellent storyteller." Adeline sat on the edge of Josiah's bed. "But I don't know that story. Do you want to tell it to me?"

"Sure." Josiah bounced up and sat on his knees. "Once upon a time—"

"Lay back down." The last thing she needed was for the bedtime story to hype him up and make it harder for him to go to sleep. "You can tell me the story just fine with your head on your pillow."

"Um…'kay."

She held up the covers, and he squirmed underneath them until he was comfortable. "Once upon a time," he started again, "there was a sailor who sailed the seven seas to protect his country. He loved his job and his country, but he didn't feel appreciated."

"That's because people who joined the navy after him got the better jobs. His boss told him he wasn't smart enough to be a leader," Matthew added. He'd placed his book back on his bed's headboard shelf and rolled onto his side to face them.

"Hey, I'm telling this story." Josiah glared at his brother.

"Then don't leave out the good parts." Matthew smirked and tucked his arm under his head.

"All right boys. No need to argue. It's okay if you both tell the story." She turned back to Josiah. "Matthew was only trying to help, so I'll know the story and can tell it to you correctly next time."

"I guess." He looked down and sighed.

"Scooch over." Matthew hopped out of his bed, dove into Josiah's, then crawled under the covers with his brother. "She's right, you know. If we want her to tell us the story the way Dad told it, we can't skip anything."

"Then we gotta do the acting parts!"

"Yeah!"

Before she could stop them, both boys jumped out of bed and ran to the center of the room. Matthew dug into the toy chest at the foot of his bed until he found a pirate's hat, sword and an eye patch. He handed everything to Josiah, who quickly put the costume on. Then he pulled out a sailor's cap and slipped on a pair of dark sunglasses.

"Matthew… Josiah… Boys!" The twins were so engrossed in their mission, her pleas went unheard.

A whistle rent the air. The twins looked up and froze. Adeline turned to see Linc standing in the doorway, his thumb and forefinger between his lips. He met her gaze and shrugged before turning to the boys. "Answer your aunt when she's calling your name."

"Yes, sir," they said in unison and turned to her, crestfallen expressions on their faces. "Sorry, Aunt Addie."

"We only wanted to tell the story the way Dad did," Matthew mumbled.

"Yeah, that's all," Josiah added.

Their hurt expressions were her undoing. She didn't have the heart to tell them no. Even though she knew allowing them to put on a full show right before bed would wire them up, and it would take longer for them to fall asleep.

"Promise me, after you finish the story, you'll go straight to bed. And stay there. No getting up until morning," she said in a stern voice.

"Yay!" they cheered, and then dove back into the toy chest and pulled out a few more items, placing them on the floor behind the chest so she couldn't see them.

The mattress gave as Linc sat next to her on the edge of Josiah's bed. "Mind if I stay for the show?"

"Not if you teach me how to whistle like that," she whispered.

He chuckled and leaned closer. "Any time."

His woodsy cologne wafted over her, and her heart skipped a beat as she realized having him near brought her a sense of safety and peace she hadn't felt in a long time. And that thought scared her more than the man after them.

The nearness of her made him feel claustrophobic. No. That wasn't it. If it was claustrophobia, he'd be trying to find an escape. This was more of a hyperawareness of her presence, the fragrance of her vanilla-scented shampoo and the overwhelming desire to pull her closer.

"Ahem." He cleared his throat. "I'd forgotten how tiny twin beds were. I didn't mean to crowd you."

Linc moved to the other bed and sat against the headboard with his legs stretched out and his arms crossed over his chest. "So, what's the play they're putting on?"

Adeline gave him a quizzical look then settled back on the other bed in a move that mimicked his. "It's a bedtime story Isaac made up. It's one of the last ones he told them. Josiah wanted to hear it, but since I didn't know it, they're teaching it to me. This is the story of *The Pirate and the Princess*."

"Okay, we're ready." Matthew commanded their attention.

"Once upon a time…" Josiah began. "There was a sailor who sailed the seven seas to protect his country. He loved his job and his country, but he didn't feel appreciated because people who joined the navy after him got the better jobs. When he asked his boss about it, the sailor was told he wasn't smart enough to be a leader.

"Then a new commander was assigned to his ship. The sailor and the commander became friends. The sailor nicknamed his new friend Copper Penny because the commander had copper-colored hair and a shiny personality. Copper constantly praised the sailor, and he became puffed up." Josiah inhaled sharply and stuck out his chest. Holding his breath a tad too long, he exhaled with a cough. "Soon, the sailor thought he was invisible—"

"Invincible, not invisible," Matthew interrupted. "People could see him."

"Oh, that's right. Invincible." Josiah leaned toward Adeline and Linc and whispered, "That means he thinks nothing can hurt him."

The boys were entertaining. Linc swallowed the laughter that tickled the back of his throat. This was the first time they'd seemed comfortable around him. He couldn't hurt their feelings by appearing to laugh at them.

"Thanks for clarifying." Adeline smiled and motioned for the boys to continue.

Matthew took over the storytelling. "The sailor didn't know that Copper was really a pirate. Copper only pretended to be his friend to steal a big treasure, but the sailor didn't know what was happening until it was too late. When the sailor told Copper he didn't want to be a pirate, Copper threatened to tell the police the sailor stole the treasure. Copper convinced the sailor the only way to avoid punishment was to become a pirate, too. Then Copper would help protect his identity. The sailor decided being a pirate was better than going to jail. As a pirate he could control which secrets were sold and which ones were protected. So, the sailor became a pirate. He stole top-secret treasures and gave them to Copper to sell to other countries for lots of gold. This went on for years. With each passing year, the sailor became more comfortable being a pirate and he feared his heart was becoming hardened."

"Then one day," Josiah said, "the pirate met a beautiful brown-haired princess. She was sweet and honest, and she saw the good in everyone. Even the pirate. The more he was around her, the more he fell in love. But there was a problem. Princesses didn't marry pirates. The only way he could make her his bride was to give up being a pirate. That also meant giving up his life as a sailor, too. So, he quit his job.

"Copper was furious and threatened to turn the pirate over to the police. The pirate would go to prison for stealing his country's secrets and would never be able to marry the princess. The pirate gathered all his courage and told Copper if he went to jail, Copper would, too. The pirate had proof Copper was behind the crimes. He was willing to turn Copper in even if it meant he would go to prison for his crimes, too. Because if he couldn't be with the princess, he had no life at all. This angered Copper. But the pirate made a deal with Copper. As long as Copper left him and the princess alone, he'd keep the evidence hidden, but if Copper ever became a threat to him or his new family, he'd turn over the evidence and they'd both go to jail."

Matthew stepped forward. "The threat worked. Copper sailed away, leaving the pirate and the princess in peace. As he promised, the pirate hid the proof he had against Copper in a treasure chest and placed it near his favorite body of water. Then he turned the key to the chest into a neckless for his princess. So, the pirate and the princess got married. They had two little princes, and they were the happiest family in all the land.

"Sometimes the pirate would hear stories that Copper was still taking treasures from the government and selling them for gold, but he wouldn't let fear of Copper's illegal activities ruin his happy life. As long as the key was hidden close to the princess's heart, the pirate's family would remain safe."

"And they all lived happily-ever-after," Josiah said, his voice cracking. "But happily-ever-after is just for fairy tales. In real life, people die and leave their children behind."

Sobbing, he dove into Adeline's arms. She whispered soothing words as she tried to calm him.

Linc wanted to offer words of wisdom but knew there weren't any words he could say to take away the sting of losing parents. No matter the age, it wasn't an easy thing to process.

Several minutes later, Josiah's sobs turned to hiccups. He sat up and wiped his face with his pajama top. Matthew looped his arm through his twin's. "Brother, why don't we have an indoor campout tonight?"

"Indoor campout. What's that?" Adeline asked.

"That's when boys make a tent out of blankets and sleep on the floor." Linc thought of his own indoor campouts as a child. A pang of sadness pierced him. He hadn't had a brother to share the experience with, but Jessica had always been his little shadow and usually ended up falling asleep in his makeshift tent before their dad moved her to her own bed. Seven years and, though he'd learned to mask it, the pain of losing his sister was as strong as it had been the day he'd received the call about her murder. He shook his head and forced his mind back to the present. The boys were explaining to their aunt how to make the tent.

"The cover stretches between the two beds." Matthew reached for the top cover on his bed, so Linc scooted off the bed and stood to the side.

Josiah motioned for Adeline to vacate his bed and then lifted the top corner of the mattress. "See, we tuck it under here."

"Here, we'll help. Addie, you and Josiah lift his mattress and I'll get Matthew's." Linc crossed to Matthew's side and lifted the mattress so Matthew could tuck the edge of the blanket underneath it. Soon the blanket was stretched taut between the beds, with all the pillows and additional blankets piled on the floor underneath it.

Matthew crossed to the closet and came back with a small battery-powered lantern. "All set. You and Linc can go now, Aunt Addie. Don't forget to turn the lights out."

Adeline reached down and kissed the top of each boy's head. "Don't stay up too late telling campfire stories. And watch out for tigers and bears."

Both boys groaned at the joke, and Linc chuckled. "Good night, boys."

An unfamiliar yearning tugged at his heart as he clicked off the light, closed the boys' bedroom door and followed Addie into the hall. He felt a sudden, profound sense of loss for the children he would never have. Although he'd first doubted family life was for him after witnessing so many soldiers die in combat, the idea had been cemented into his mind while building his and Ryan's business into one of the most respected private security firms in the nation. Eighty-hour weeks left little time for a family. But that was okay because Protective Instincts *was* his baby and his employees were his family. That was all he needed.

Yeah, right.

NINE

"Now that the boys are settled, I think we should start searching through the files in the office. After all, that's where the intruder went last night. Obviously, he thought he'd find what he was looking for in there." A thought struck, and Adeline stopped midway down the stairs and turned to look up at Linc. "How did the intruder know the location of Isaac's office? He must have been inside this house before. Could he be one of Isaac's friends or a colleague?"

"Most likely," Linc concurred. "Do you know if Vanessa and Isaac often entertained work colleagues in their home?"

"No." She puffed out a breath, turned and sprinted down the remaining steps. "I hate to admit it, but I'm not even sure what Isaac did for a living."

"I say if he wasn't a children's book author, he missed the mark. That was some tale the boys just shared. Who would think to combine a pirate story with a princess story?"

She smiled. "As far as bedtime stories in this house goes, that was fairly tame. Isaac and Vanessa were creative when they made up stories for the boys. I've heard stories about giant grasshoppers ridden by cowboys and invisible flying cars driven by Martians. And in case you didn't know, thunder and lightning are caused when the Martians crash their invisible cars."

"I may need to hear both of those stories sometime." Linc laughed. "And I think we need to tell Ryan and Hadley to up their game. Sophia is missing out. They only tell her the classic bedtime stories like *The Three Little Pigs* and *Cinderella*."

"There's nothing wrong with the classics. I quite prefer them myself." She crossed the threshold into the office and stopped in the middle of the room. There was a floor-to-ceiling built-in bookcase on one wall, two filing cabinets—one she'd partially looked through the night before and one she hadn't opened yet—and a desktop computer. "I don't have a clue where to start."

Linc crossed to the desk. "Is the computer password protected?"

"Yes, but it was easy to hack."

"Don't tell me he used a birthday or anniversary date?"

"No. Not quite that simple. It isn't something a random person could pull up online."

He turned to her and cocked an eyebrow. "Are you going to share?"

If it had been another place and another situation, she would have enjoyed letting him try to guess what Isaac had chosen for the passcode, to see how long it would have taken him to figure it out, but they'd wasted enough time already letting the boys tell them the bedtime story. Though she couldn't feel bad about that because it had given Matthew and Josiah a small sense of normalcy.

Adeline sat in the desk chair and booted up the computer. "Thirty-two, thirty-nine," she said as she keyed in the numbers. The computer came to life and a photo of Vanessa and Isaac holding their newborn sons flashed on the screen.

"Vanessa and Isaac's ages?"

"No. Minutes." She met her boss's gaze and knew the instant he figured out the numbers.

"The twins' times of birth?"

"Brilliant, don't you think? It's not something most people would know, but a close family member—namely me—could figure it out."

"I'm surprised *you* were able to figure it out. I don't think most aunts or uncles would remember that kind of information. Did it take you long to come up with it?"

"Actually, no. I got it on my fourth attempt. Ruling out birthdays and their wedding anniversary, this was the next obvious combination. As for knowing their times of birth, Vanessa had a cute habit of…" Her voice trailed off as it dawned on her nothing her sister or Isaac had done since she'd moved back to Denver had been by chance. They had planted seeds in her mind to prepare her for this day. For when she became guardian of the boys. Did that mean Vanessa had known her life was in danger?

"What's wrong?" Linc asked.

She shook her head. "Nothing. It's just…on the boys' birthday, Vanessa would have two cakes. Matthew, being the oldest, would blow out his candles first…at exactly 11:32 a.m., and Josiah, would blow his out seven minutes later."

"At 11:39 a.m." Linc nodded. "That explains how you knew their times of birth."

"Yes, but what if the purpose of doing their cakes that way went deeper than simply being a cute twin birthday thing? They only started doing it after I moved back from Dallas. So, they only did it twice. The boys' seventh and eighth birthdays. Vanessa told me once that Isaac had come up with the idea. She'd thought it was so sweet of him to think of something like that. And it was. But what if he did it so I would figure out the passcode to his computer?"

She furrowed her brow. "He and Vanessa had detailed wills with copies of their insurance policies and burial requests stored in a fireproof lockbox in the closet in this room. Last Thanksgiving, they gave me and Mom the only keys to that box and told us not to lose them. We both thought they were going a bit overboard, but since they had young children, it seemed only natural for their affairs to be in order. So, we accepted the keys to put their minds at ease, never dreaming we'd need them a few months later."

"Why not just put the passcode for the computer, along with any other important passwords, in the lockbox for you to find?"

"Maybe Isaac was afraid of the lockbox being stolen or broken into."

"Wills and insurance policies, while important, are replaceable. But you think whatever is on that computer isn't. Or at least it isn't something that needs to fall into the hands of just anyone."

"Exactly. I also can't help but wonder what other clues Isaac and Vanessa planted in my memories that I've overlooked." She fisted her hands and her fingernails bit into her palms. "I keep replaying the night of the accident in my mind. Isaac asked me if I could watch the boys. He wanted to take Vanessa out for their anniversary. Their actual anniversary wasn't for two more weeks. I figured, since they had kids and his work schedule could be unpredictable, he was trying to fit in a romantic date night while he could and they'd celebrate on their actual anniversary with a dinner at home with the boys."

"But now you think something else was going on…" Linc dropped into an armchair on the other side of the desk. "Talk me through your thoughts. Maybe together we can figure out what your brother-in-law was up to."

"I keep remembering how nervous Vanessa seemed. She kept hugging and kissing the boys. And she told me at least four times where they were having dinner and what time they'd be home. She emphasized that they would not be late. It was as if she'd never left the boys with a babysitter before, and it wasn't like I was a sitter here for the first time. I'm their aunt. I'd stayed with them many times since moving back. The boys even spent the night at my condo a few times." She bit her lip. "I offered to take them to my place for the night so Vanessa and Isaac wouldn't have to cut their romantic evening short, but she was adamant that they had to stay here. She said she'd want to see them and hug them the minute the evening was over."

Linc whistled softly. "I'm not a parent—and I've never babysat for anyone—but that sounds odd. Almost as if she hadn't been looking forward to the evening out with her husband. Do you think they got into a fight before you arrived? Could that explain her behavior?"

"No." Adeline shook her head. "I never witnessed them arguing. When they were getting ready to leave, Isaac helped Vanessa into her coat and they embraced for several minutes, with him kissing the top of her head and whispering something to her."

She gasped and jumped up, knocking the desk chair

over. "I forgot about Isaac's parting words." Her mind raced as she struggled to process the thoughts forming in her brain.

"What did he say?" Linc materialized by her side and turned her to face him.

"He emphasized I shouldn't forget the boys' bedtime routine, especially story time. And instead of reading the boys a bedtime story, I'd probably want to let them tell me the new one he'd been teaching them."

Adeline and Linc's eyes locked. *"The Pirate and the Princess!"* they exclaimed in unison.

"Quick. We need to write the story down, so we don't forget anything." Adeline bent to pick up a notepad and pen off the desk, and the window behind her exploded. A bullet whizzed over her head.

"Get down!" Linc yelled and pulled her to the floor as a barrage of bullets drilled holes into the wall. They belly-crawled around the mahogany desk, using it as a barrier.

"I have to get upstairs to the boys."

Linc scooted to the window, gun in hand. "Go! I'll cover you."

A long-forgotten childhood memory flashed through her mind of her and Vanessa crawling into their parents' bed during a thunderstorm and her mom telling them not to be afraid because *God will cover us with His wings and will protect us from the storms.*

She pushed to her feet and ran with all her might as gunshots rang out behind her. *God, please, cover Linc as he puts himself in harm's way.*

The boys met her at the top of the stairs. "Aunt Addie!"

"Why are they shooting at us?"

"I'm scared!"

"Make it stop!"

Adeline scooped both boys up into her arms, and they burrowed their faces in her neck. "It's going to be okay." But only if she could get them into a safe location. The master bedroom closet was the most interior room on the top floor. Shifting the boys' weight so she could reach the doorknob, she crossed into the room she'd been avoiding for the past week.

After depositing the boys on the floor, she opened the door to the spacious walk-in closet, flipped on the light switch and herded them inside. She hadn't seen the inside of the closet since Vanessa had given her the grand tour, after she and Isaac purchased the house seven years ago. What had once been a large, empty space was filled with custom built-ins and a steel gun safe that stood six feet tall. It would be a perfect shield.

"Here. Sit on the floor beside this."

Without time to wonder what her brother-in-law had kept inside the safe, she got the boys into position beside it.

She knelt on the floor in front of them. "I need you both to stay here. I've got to go—"

"No! Don't leave us." Josiah dove into her arms.

Adeline pried his little arms from around her neck and settled him back beside Matthew. "I have to. Linc needs my help. Please, stay here until I come back for you."

"Yes, Aunt Addie." Matthew pulled Josiah into a hug. "Go. We'll wait here."

For once, she was thankful for his pretend bravado. She kissed the tops of both boys' heads and raced out of the room, locking the bedroom door and pulling it closed behind her. It wouldn't stop anyone from getting inside, but it would slow them down. And she would be there until her last breath, fighting to protect her nephews.

Lord, I messed up. I should have immediately moved them to a safer location. Don't let them pay the ultimate price for my error in judgment. Please, cover them with Your wings.

The sound of sirens pierced the air, and the shooting from outside stopped. A car door slammed and tires squalled. Linc looked out the window as the silhouette of a car that looked like the one that had nearly run them over this morning disappeared into the night. A police cruiser chased after it as a second cruiser pulled into the drive.

A gasp sounded from the doorway, and he turned to see Adeline, the color draining from her face as she took in the damage to the office, the shattered windows and bullet-hole-ridden walls.

There was a loud bang on the front door. "Police!"

Adeline stared, transfixed on the wreckage inside the room. "Do you think they'll believe me this time, that this isn't a random attack?"

"Only one way to find out." Linc slid his weapon into his shoulder holster and pulled his shirt down over it.

"Can you let them in?" she asked as she started up the stairs. "I left the boys in the master bedroom closet. I want to let them know everything is okay and they can go back to their room if they want."

The pounding sounded again. "Police! Is everyone okay?"

He opened the door to the same officers who had responded to last night's break-in. "Everyone's fine. Just shaken. Please, come in. Adeline has gone to check on the twins, but she'll be down shortly."

Forty-five minutes later, after taking their statements and notifying them the shooter had gotten away, the officers left with a promise to drive past the house in regular intervals overnight. Linc locked the door, reset the alarm and crossed the foyer to the office. Plywood covered the windows, thanks to Ryan, Zane and Lucy who had all showed up minutes after the police.

Ryan came up behind him. "The plywood was the best we could do tonight. I'll start making calls in the morning to get new windows installed ASAP."

"Thank you for rushing back over here." Linc looked at his best friend and sent up a silent prayer of thanks for their special bond.

"No problem. When the security monitoring service called and said the alarm was going off and they couldn't get anyone to answer, I figured you could use backup. You would have done the same for me. Actually, you've had my back more times than I can count." Ryan chuckled. "At least I didn't have to drive three hundred and fifty miles in a blizzard like you did to be there for me and Hadley when Sophia was kidnapped."

Linc would never forget the terror Ryan and Hadley had gone through after Sophia had been kidnapped. He had been thankful to be there for them and to support them during that time of crisis. It had amazed Linc how attached Ryan had become to Sophia in such a short amount of time, but now he understood all too well how quickly protective feelings could surge when a child was in danger. When the abductor had snatched Matthew at the zoo, Linc had been desperate to rescue him, and Matthew had only been out of their sights for a few seconds before they located him and got him back.

"We make a good team."

"Yes, we do." Ryan clapped him on the shoulder and headed toward the kitchen, where Zane and Lucy waited for instructions.

Time to find Adeline. The person after them was getting more aggressive, and they needed to discuss their next move. Linc understood why she wanted to keep the boys in their own home, but it was too dangerous. She had to realize that.

He paused in the living room doorway. Matthew and Josiah were curled up on the sofa, sound asleep. When Adeline had come down the stairs earlier with the twins in tow, she'd told them they could stay as long as they sat quietly. If they couldn't, she would send them back upstairs to their room. They had agreed and huddled together on one corner of the sofa with a throw blanket. Periodically they'd whispered something to each other, but never loud enough to be a disturbance. It seemed they had finally given in to their exhaustion. Good. Maybe, now that they were sleeping, he could have a conversation with Adeline about moving them to a safe house without worrying about little ears overhearing. Linc just hoped she wouldn't fight him on the decision.

The sound of someone coming down the stairs drew his attention. He glanced up and saw Adeline approaching with two backpacks. He met her at the foot of the stairs. "What's this?"

"Clothes and a few toys for the boys. I still need to grab their devices so they can log in to their school accounts and complete assignments, but this should last them a few days."

"Good. It looks like we're thinking along the same lines. If you want to grab the devices and your things, I'll let Ryan know you need an escort to the safe house. Lucy can stay with you tonight and then we'll figure out a schedule for the rest of the week."

She dropped the backpacks she'd been holding and started at him, openmouthed. "I'm not going anywhere. The boys are. I'm staying here until I find what this creep is looking for. It's obvious Isaac was involved in something illegal, and I intend to find out what it was."

"So, you're going to send the boys off to a safe house with someone they don't know?"

"Only overnight. I trust all my coworkers. Don't you?" She turned and headed down the hallway.

"Yes. Of course, I do," he said, trailing after her to the mudroom. "But what do you mean 'only overnight'? Does this mean you'll go to the safe house in the morning even if we've not found what we're looking for?"

"No. What it means is I called my mother while I was upstairs packing the boys' clothes. She's booking a flight as we speak and will arrive in Denver tomorrow morning." Adeline picked up the boys' school bags from the bench where they'd tossed them earlier, carried them to the foyer and placed them on the floor beside the backpacks. "I would appreciate it if you could arrange for someone to pick her up and transport her to the safe house."

She met his gaze, her eyes pleading with him. "I know it's not an ideal situation, but I can't have the boys feeling abandoned. And I was afraid if we sent the boys to

Florida, the shooter would follow them. Maybe this way, we can keep what's left of my family safe from harm."

As much as he wanted to argue with her, and tell her she was being stubborn, he couldn't. If he were in her shoes, he would've done things the same way. "Okay, then. Sounds like you've thought everything through. I'll have Zane and Lucy take the boys to—"

"No need," Ryan said, coming down the hall toward them, Zane and Lucy right behind him. "The boys and I bonded this afternoon. I'll take them and Gunther to my house for the night. Then I can transport them to the safe house after picking up Adeline's mom from the airport."

"I can't let you put your family in danger that way." Adeline looked at Ryan aghast.

"You're not *letting* me do anything. As co-owner of Protective Instincts, *and your boss*, I'm taking over the protective duties of guarding those young boys… Unless you want to go with them to the safe house…? In which case, I'll stay here and help Linc look for clues." Ryan crossed his arms over his chest and waited.

When there was no reply, he unfolded his arms and smiled. "I promise you, I wouldn't do anything to put my wife and daughter in danger. If I didn't think I could get the boys to my house undetected by the shooter, I'd never take the chance. However, I know I can. And I believe the boys will feel a little more relaxed with Sophia around. She has a way of making people smile and forget their troubles."

"Aunt Addie." Matthew stood in the living room opening. "I didn't mean to listen to a grown-up conversation. But your voices woke me." He ran to Adeline and threw his arms around her. "We'll go with Mr. Ryan, and I promise Josiah and I will behave. But promise me you and Linc will catch the guy doing all this, and you won't let him kill you."

Tears flowed down Matthew's cheeks. Adeline sank to the floor and held him as his body shook, releasing all the tears and emotions he'd bottled up since his parents' deaths.

Lord, darkness is fighting to engulf this family. You are the light, and with You guiding us, I know we can overcome evil. Please, keep this family safe. They've already experienced so much pain. Help them heal and give Adeline the confidence to raise these boys as her own. Help her see she needs them as much as they need her.

The urge to run away with Adeline and the twins to a remote island where evil could not touch them vibrated through Linc's body. He fisted his hands at his sides as he fought to tamp down this foreign desire to protect them as if they were his own family. He'd have to examine his tangled emotions when this was all over, but for now he'd focus on finding the shooter.

TEN

Twenty minutes after Ryan and the twins left, Adeline stood inside the master bedroom closet with Linc, frustration bubbling up inside her after three failed attempts to open the gun safe. Biting her lip, she leaned in to try once more.

"I've tried the boys' birth times and birth date, and Vanessa and Isaac's wedding anniversary." A strand of hair fell into her face. She puffed out a breath of air and blew it away. "Let's try Vanessa's birth date." She punched in the six-digit combination and the safe emitted a long, harsh beeping sound. She'd failed again. "Ugh. I don't know what the combination could be. I'm pretty sure I'll only have one more attempt before we're locked out."

"You're probably right. Most safes like this will allow up to five attempts before going on lockdown for fifteen to twenty minutes. If we don't get it open on the next attempt, we'll have to go back downstairs to the office and search through the files on the computer while we wait."

The annoying strand of hair fell across her eyes, again. Adeline sighed and went into the bathroom. She yanked open the vanity drawers until she located a hair tie. Gathering her long, wavy hair in a high ponytail, she looped the tie around it several times and, on the third pass, only pulled her hair halfway through the tie. A quick glance in the mirror showed she'd created a messy bun atop her head. She wouldn't win any beauty pageants with the hairstyle, but it would keep her hair out of her eyes as she worked. The sight of Linc's reflection in the mirror caught her attention. Leaning against the door frame and staring at her, he probably thought she'd not only lost her cool but also her mind, fixing her hair at this critical moment.

She pointed to her head. "Just trying to keep the hair out of my eyes so I can concentrate."

He nodded. "Jessica used to do the same thing when she was studying. She said it was like putting on a *thinking cap*. It helped her focus."

"You don't talk about your sister much. When I first signed on at Protective Instincts, I didn't realize your sister and Ryan's murdered fiancée was the same person."

"The less I dwelled on what had happened, the easier it was to keep going. I knew Jessica would want Ryan and me to start our business and make it successful. So, I put all my energy into building something my little sister would be proud of." He straightened. "Of course, I'm glad Ryan pursued justice and caught the man who killed Jessica. He has the closure he needed and has moved on with his life."

"That's what I want to give the twins. Closure. I have to find out the truth about what happened to them. And stop the person after us. Then I can concentrate on selling this house and moving the boys to Florida to live with my parents."

He lifted on eyebrow. "I know it's not any of my business, but I wonder if that's what the boys want. Moving to

Florida. It's not what your sister wanted, or she wouldn't have named you guardian."

He was right. It *wasn't* any of his business. Of course, she'd never tell him that. Being confrontational, especially with those in authority—like her employer or supervisor— was not part of her DNA. He meant well, but she would not engage in a discussion about her responsibilities regarding the twins. If the past twenty-four hours had done nothing else, it had highlighted her ineptness as a substitute parent. Besides, even if she wanted to hear Linc's thoughts on the subject, she didn't have time to waste. Brushing past him, she entered the closet and stood in front of the safe once more. "I haven't tried Isaac's birth date, but I'm hesitant to try it since none of the other birthdays worked."

"I agree. Since he used the twins' birth times for his computer code, this code will probably be something unique," Linc said. "Can you think of any other quirky habits Isaac had that involved numbers? You said earlier that it felt like he and Vanessa had been planting clues to help you figure out passwords. Was there anything he said to you, more than once, that involved numbers that stuck with you?"

"He liked to tease me. How I was moving up in the world."

Linc nodded. "Because Denver is the Mile High City."

"Yes. Isaac also made up a jingle of sorts that he would recite in a singsong voice every time he saw me for the first couple of months after my move." She furrowed her brow. "Let's see, how did it go? Little sis is moving up in the world. Leaving behind oil wells for mountains of gold. Climbing to the top of the Mile High City. She won't regret exchanging the 214 for the 303."

"*Exchanging the 214 for the 303...* I don't get it."

"My Dallas area code and their Denver area code." Adeline gasped. "Six digits. That's it!"

She inhaled deeply then slowly exhaled. She punched in the code. Two rapid beeps sounded. She held her breath, turned the knob and pulled. The door popped open, and she yelled for joy. "I did it!"

"Way to go!" Linc swept her up and swung her around, then put her down and stepped backward. "Um, I'm sorry. Got caught up in the moment."

So had she. The stress of multiple failures had intensified the joy when she'd entered the correct code. She mumbled a quick "no worries" and opened the safe door wider, eager to look inside and to change the subject.

The contents of the safe consisted of a large accordion-style file organizer, two rifles, three handguns and multiple stacks of ammo.

Linc peered over her shoulder. "Considering the size of the safe, I was expecting more. Maybe some jewels. Diamonds and emeralds and pearls."

"It would have shocked me if we had found jewels. Mom convinced Vanessa to do beauty pageants in high school to earn scholarships for college. Vanessa always finished in the top three, and earned several scholarships, but she never won the title of Queen. After the fourth or fifth pageant, she told mom she was done. She'd never been into all the glitz and glamour that went along with pageants. After that, other than her wedding rings, the only jewelry Vanessa ever wore was a pair of simple stud earrings and a necklace Isaac gave her." She pulled the file box out of the safe and sat on the floor to go through it.

Linc's cell phone buzzed, and he looked at the screen. "It's a text from Ryan. They made it to his house without any trouble. He's sure no one followed them. Matthew and Josiah are already sound asleep, with Gunther at the foot of their bed standing guard. As an extra precaution, Zane and Lucy are staying and will accompany them and your mom to the safe house tomorrow."

Before joining Protective Instincts four months ago, Zane worked as a SWAT team member. Knowing he and Lucy were there to offer assistance, if needed, helped ease her worries. "I appreciate the steps they're taking to protect the boys. Tell Ryan thanks."

He typed a response and hit Send. Slipping his phone into his back pocket, he eased onto the floor beside her. "Find anything important?"

"Not yet." Adeline thumbed through the index labels. "Investment Portfolio. Lake House. Life Insurance. Twins' Health Records. Wait a minute…" Going back to the section labeled Lake House, she pulled out the deed for the vacation home her sister and Isaac had purchased three years ago. Included in the file were photos of the single-story log cabin and the boathouse that sheltered Isaac's boat.

"I forgot about their vacation home." The memory of Isaac's excitement when he'd showed her the lake house hit like a bolt of lightning. He'd said being on his boat with his family on *beautiful Lake Granby* was his favorite place to be. She gasped. "The clue to what the intruder is looking for is in the bedtime story."

"Are you sure?" Linc tilted his head, a frown tugging at the corners of his mouth.

"Positive. The story was about a sailor. Isaac joined the navy right out of high school."

"What about the pirate part? In the story, the sailor became a pirate. Do you think your brother-in-law was capable of treason?"

"Of course." A startled expression crossed Linc's face and she rushed to clarify. "Isaac was a great guy. A loving husband and father, and a welcoming brother-in-law. If I find out he was involved in anything illegal, it will surprise me. But I won't think less of him. Because I believe all people, no matter how good of a person they are, are capable of breaking the law given the right circumstances. And they are also redeemable."

He nodded. "I agree with that. So, let's solve the riddle of *The Pirate and the Princess*."

Adeline pushed to her feet and stepped out into the master bedroom. If she was going to figure this out, it would require some serious pacing and thinking. "Okay, so, the sailor—Isaac—met a pirate who convinced him to steal navy secrets and sell them to other countries. But then he met the princess—Vanessa—and decided he wanted to marry her and leave behind his life of crime."

"But not before gathering evidence against Copper," Linc added as he strode to the only chair in the room. He moved Vanessa's Denver Broncos sweatshirt off the seat and draped it across the arm, then sat and faced Adeline.

Anger that he dared to touch anything in the room swelled inside her. The command *Get up and put the sweatshirt back* crawled up her throat and begged to be released. She swallowed her annoyance. Leaving the sweatshirt in the chair wouldn't bring her sister back. Eventually, she would have to put aside the desire to leave the room as it was the last time Vanessa had been in it, and box up her sister's belongings, choosing which items to donate to charity and which items to put away for the boys to have.

Focus. She met his eyes. "He hid the evidence— treasure—near his favorite body of water."

"The lake house," they said in unison.

"The pirate made the key to the treasure into a neck- lace for his princess." Adeline rushed to the dresser and opened the small top center drawer, where she had put Vanessa's jewelry the hospital had given her after the ac- cident. "The necklace Isaac gave to Vanessa on their hon- eymoon. Why didn't I think of it sooner?"

She pulled the chain out of the drawer and turned to show Linc, who had come to stand beside her. A silver key with the words *all we need* stamped, in lowercase letters, on the bow dangled from the end of a white gold chain, along with three tag charms stamped with the words *Va- nessa & Isaac, Matthew, Josiah,* and a small diamond- encrusted heart. Upon closer inspection, it was obvious the key she had thought was another charm was, indeed, an actual key. "The answer was here the entire time. Isaac thought of everything."

"We still have to figure out where he hid the box this key fits. Our treasure hunt may be far from over."

"True. We'll just have to think it through once we get to Lake Granby."

Linc checked his smartwatch. "It's nearing midnight. Do you want to go now, or should we try to sleep and leave at sunup?"

"I'm not waiting until morning. It would be a waste of

time. There's no way I'd ever be able to shut my mind off and fall asleep right now."

"I figured as much. Okay, it's probably a good idea for us both to be armed since we're not sure what we'll find once we get there. Grab your gun. I'll put everything back into the safe and text Ryan to let him know where we're headed."

She closed her fist around the necklace and impulsively threw both arms around Linc's waist. "Thank you. For all that you are doing and have done to help me keep the boys safe."

He wrapped his arms around her. "I wouldn't want to be anywhere else," he whispered near her ear.

As crazy as it seemed, during a time when she was running from someone trying to kill her, she had never felt safer than she did at that moment in his arms. Frightened by the thought, she pulled away from him, mumbled, "I'll be right back," and raced out of the room. Once inside the guestroom where she'd been sleeping, she closed the door and leaned against it.

Taking measured deep breaths, she willed her heart to slow to a normal rate. It was common to have confused, mixed-up feelings for someone who was being supportive during a difficult time. Just like one didn't need to sign contracts or make life-altering decisions following a traumatic event, it was also imperative not to give in to feelings of attraction during a crisis. Adeline knew, just like she wasn't cut out to be a mom, she would never be a wife. So, even if Linc wasn't her boss, a romantic relationship was not in the forecast for her life.

Exhaling one last deep breath, she crossed to the closet and pulled her small lockbox off the top shelf. Time was wasting. They needed to get to the lake house and find the information to identify Copper and put him away, so he could never threaten the boys' lives again.

ELEVEN

After gathering the papers Adeline had left on the floor of the closet and putting them back into the accordion file, Linc placed it on the shelf in the gun safe. He considered taking one of the handguns for a backup, but thought better of it. He and Adeline were armed, so they wouldn't need another weapon. He closed the door and double-checked to ensure it had locked.

"Ready to go?" Adeline yelled from the hall.

He met her at the top of the stairs. She wore a pair of hiking boots and a down jacket, and she had changed her messy bun into a sleek ponytail. The necklace hung around her neck, and the key rested against her chest.

"I thought I'd be less likely to lose it if I wore it." She pulled the chain up and slipped the key underneath her shirt.

"Good idea," he mumbled, embarrassed Addie had caught him staring. Linc cleared his throat. "I'm glad you thought to grab a heavy coat. Being farther north and at a higher elevation, Granby is usually colder than Denver, especially in mid April."

"Yeah, that's what I thought." She eyed him. "Isaac's winter jacket is hanging in the entryway, if you want to wear it."

"Thanks. You said you've been to the lake house before. Will we have trouble finding it in the dark? Are there a lot of neighbors close by?"

"I've been twice. There are neighbors. Some live there year-round and others, like Isaac and Vanessa, are only there on the occasional weekend and holidays. However, none of the houses are close. The developer sectioned the land into three- to four-acre lots and planted trees along the borders of the properties to provide the most secluded feeling possible for the residents.

"Oh, I almost forgot." She dashed into the master bedroom and then returned with a set of keys dangling from one finger. "We'll need the key when we get to the lake house. Let's go."

They jogged down the stairs. Adeline deactivated the alarm and reached for the front door handle. He placed a hand on her arm. "Where are you going?"

"We'll take my vehicle." Adeline shrugged him off and headed outside. "I already have the address programed into my GPS. It'll make it much easier to find the lake house in the dark."

Dumbfounded that she took off without waiting to see what his thoughts were, he stood stock-still. Linc wasn't used to being relegated to a subordinate position in situations like this, but he had to admit her reasoning sounded logical.

Get a grip, man. This isn't your normal security detail. And Adeline isn't your typical client. Actually, she's not a client at all. She's an employee. And, hopefully, from this point forward, a friend. Remember Ryan's advice. Listen and don't assume you're the one in charge all the time.

A stern shake of his head cleared his mind, and he headed out the way she'd just gone. "Wait for me!"

He stepped off the porch and froze. An icy chill crept up his spine, wrapped around his chest and gripped his heart. A muscular man with red hair stood at the edge of the driveway, his arm around Adeline's neck and a gun aimed at her temple. *Copper.* Linc reached for his weapon.

"Don't even think about it," Copper ordered, his voice frighteningly soft. "I won't hesitate to kill her. And while I know it would seal my death warrant because you'd get the next round off and kill me before I could take you out, too, I have nothing to lose. Death is less scary than facing the possibility that the information I'm looking for becomes public. So, what do you say? I kill her, then you kill me. And we're done..."

Linc clinched his teeth. His jaw muscle twitched. *Lord, help me. Guide me.* "No. We'll do things your way, Copper."

"You've started putting things together." Adeline's captor laughed. "But I prefer to be called Red. Now, take your gun out of your holster, put it on the ground and kick it to me."

Stall for time. Dear Lord, please let Mrs. McCall call nine-one-one. "Man, you've watched too many movies. I'm not kicking a loaded weapon."

Red tightened his arm around Adeline's neck and she winced.

Linc held up his hands, palms out. "What if I put my gun down and then back away so you can get it?"

"I guess that will work. Also, throw your phone behind the shrubs next to the house."

Linc pulled the gun from his holster and knelt to place it on the ground, wondering if he could communicate a secret message to Adeline and they could take the guy out. No. His military training had instilled in him not to act rashly. *Be patient for the right opening to take out the enemy.* He stood, pulled his cell out of his pocket and tossed it. It hit the brick foundation and fell behind the shrubbery. Once he completed the assigned tasks, Linc took three big steps backward.

"Farther," Red demanded.

He nodded and took three more steps backward as Red and Adeline came closer. They reached the spot where he'd left the gun, and Red shoved Adeline into Linc and bent to retrieve the weapon.

Linc stumbled and locked his arms around Adeline as he fought to keep them both upright. "Are you okay?"

She bobbed her head. "He got the jump on me. Took my gun and my phone."

"It's okay."

"Isn't this a touching scene?" Red laughed.

They broke apart and turned to see Red's gun trained on them.

"You know, if you shoot us, the neighbors will hear the commotion and call the police," Linc said with what he hoped sounded like more bravado than he felt. There was something about looking down the barrel of a gun that seemed to erase all of his training. All he could think of was that he needed to buy time until he could figure out how to keep Adeline safe. "I'd be surprised if someone hasn't already called in a report of a man lurking around. After the break-in last night, followed by shots fired earlier tonight, people are on high alert."

"If my shots had hit their marks earlier, there'd be no need for additional ones now." Red lifted his gun higher and pointed it at Linc's head. "But it's okay, because we're going to be long gone before the police arrive. I believe Adeline said something about going to a lake house. If you're headed there in the middle of the night, I imagine you've figured out where the documents are that I want. Now, come on. Both of you, into the Jeep. Jameson will drive, and Adeline will sit in the passenger's seat, right in front of me and my gun."

Linc narrowed his eyes. Red knew their names. He'd done his homework.

"That's right," Red sneered. "I know all about you. *Mr. Lincoln Jameson*. Co-owner of the security firm Protective Instincts and former marine. I always like to know who my adversaries are."

Adeline locked eyes with Linc. He read strength and determination in her expression. Like him, she would wait patiently for an opening and together they'd find a way out of this situation. The calm he'd struggled to find since stepping outside and seeing Adeline with a gun pointed to her head settled over him. No matter what it took, he would do whatever was required to get her out of this alive. The twins needed her. And he'd never forgive himself if anything happened to her. For the first time since they'd lost Jessica, he understood what had driven Ryan to spend every free moment hunting down her killer.

"Let's go." Red tossed Adeline's phone behind the shrub where Linc's rested and jerked his head at the Jeep.

Adeline placed her keys into Linc's palm, and he squeezed her hand, a gentle reminder they were in this together. "Patience," he said so only she could hear.

She nodded ever so slightly. "One of my better virtues."

"Stop the whispering and move," Red growled, using

his gun to herd them toward the Jeep. Both Linc's and Adeline's guns were tucked into his waistband.

For a second, Linc wondered if he could snatch one of the weapons and take down Red, but Adeline put a hand on his arm and gave a slight shake of her head. Had she had a similar thought?

Lord, please give us patience and a clear opening to stop this evil man.

"Where is this lake house?"

"In Grand County, on Lake Granby," Adeline responded.

"Three hours away," Red grumbled.

Linc pressed his lips together and stifled the retort that wanted to escape. It only took three hours when dealing with typical Denver traffic. In the middle of the night, they should make the drive in under two and a half hours. The gunman didn't need to know that. Maybe Linc could use the man's misconception to his advantage and take a little extra time to reach their destination without inciting Red. "There's no guarantee the item you're after is at the lake house. We've run out of ideas and thought we'd check it out."

"Well, you better hope it's there. If I don't find what I'm looking for tonight, it won't end well. And don't try to be a hero, either of you."

As they loaded into Adeline's Jeep, the sound of a siren in the distance broke the silence of the night. Bless Mrs. McCall. She must have alerted the police. The urge to stall their departure was strong, but Linc knew doing so would only result in a shootout in the suburban neighborhood, with many houses in close proximity. He couldn't risk an innocent person being killed by a stray bullet. Linc started the engine, put the vehicle into gear and sped out of the neighborhood before the police vehicle came into view.

Don't try to be a hero. The last words Adeline had said to Dylan right before he'd entered the convenience store, despite knowing the words had been wishful thinking even as she'd said them. After all, as police officers, they'd been in the business of doing heroic things. When they'd met at a mutual friend's birthday party, they hadn't realized they both worked for Dallas PD. With more than four thousand employees at the department, it was no surprise their paths hadn't crossed. Dylan was a detective, and Adeline was a patrol officer. They'd hit it off and, against her better judgment, had started dating.

Dylan wasn't even supposed to be at the scene the night of the robbery. When Dispatch alerted officers in the area about a robbery with hostages, Adeline and her partner had been the first to respond. Since the call had been received near the end of their shift, she'd texted Dylan, who had been waiting at a nearby barbecue place, to let him know she'd be late for their date. They'd planned to celebrate their six-month anniversary eating hot wings and watching the Cowboys' game after she got off work. Being close by, he'd decided to walk over and help with the hostage situation.

With longish, curly, dark blond hair that brushed his collar, a deep tan and crystal-blue eyes, he'd looked more like a college student who spent all his free time at the skateboard park than a police officer, and that helped him get into most places other officers couldn't. Dylan had called his superior and received permission to go into the convenience store as a customer to try to de-escalate the situation. It might have worked, if Adeline's partner, a twenty-five-year veteran, hadn't been impatient with the process. Wanting to get home to his granddaughter's first birthday party, he'd declared "enough is enough" and had gone into the store, with his gun drawn. He'd taken out the perpetrator, but not before the guy had gotten off two shots of his own—one that wounded the store clerk and the other that killed Dylan.

"Adeline... Addie..." Lincoln's voice pulled her from her thoughts.

Rubbing her temples, she pushed the pain of her past to the furthermost recesses of her mind. "Yes?"

"Are you okay? You kind of zoned out for a minute."

"Sorry."

"Stop the jabbering and enter the address into the GPS," Red ordered from the back seat.

Adeline looked over her shoulder and straight into the barrel of a gun. Red sat behind her so he could keep his gun trained on her, presumably to keep Linc in line.

"Don't think stalling until the police catch up with us will save you." Red smirked as he pierced her with emotionless blue eyes. "I know what will happen to me if they catch me. I'm willing to die. But I won't die alone. You'll both be dead before the police even have time to get out of their vehicles."

Sheer terror snaked up her spine and squeezed her lungs. *Breathe. Focus. Don't become paralyzed by fear.* What had her mom always said when Adeline was a teenager dealing with various life dramas? *Addie, always remember Proverbs 3:5. 'Trust in the Lord with all your heart. Lean not unto your own understanding.' He always has a plan. But you must let Him guide you.*

If she turned on the navigation, Red would hear the

address, eliminating his need to keep them alive. She released her breath slowly. "No need to get impatient. My boss knows how to get to Grand County from here. We're a long way from where we'll need to turn on the directions."

He pressed the barrel of the handgun to her forehead. "I said. Turn. It. On."

"Look, she's right," Linc interjected. "I know how to get to Lake Granby. We'll turn on the directions as we get closer. Having them on while we're still in the city will only be a distraction. The GPS will talk constantly, making it more difficult to focus."

"Fine. But I also know the way to Grand County. So, don't try anything funny."

"I promise. This vehicle is going to the lake house. And I won't do anything to attract law enforcement's attention." Linc reached across and squeezed her hand. She met his gaze with a subtle nod, turned back around and focused on the road ahead of them. "I want to see what's so important that you'd kill for it."

Red laughed. "You'll never see that information. It's classified."

"Oh, come on." Adeline twisted in her seat once again. "We're not naive enough to believe you'll let us live once this is over. Don't you think we at least deserve to know what we've been searching to find? So we'll know what we died for."

The gunman leaned forward, his face inches from hers. "Will knowing that make dying any easier? Will it give you comfort?"

He was playing a game with her. Taunting her. Did he want her to say yes or no? What answer would be the one that gave them more time to figure out an escape plan? *Honesty is the best policy.* More of her mother's words flashed through her mind. *No matter the situation you find yourself in. Be honest. Speak the truth. Then deal with the consequences, whatever they may be, good or bad.* "No. Knowing will not make dying easier. Nor will it comfort me. But it will answer the questions I have about my brother-in-law and what he was involved in."

"Are you sure you can handle the truth?"

"Will the truth be such a shock that it will kill me?" She scoffed. "If that's the case, I'd think you'd want me to know. It would save you a bullet."

Red roared with laughter. "I may just have to let you take a peek to see if it kills you or not." He leaned back against the seat, his gun still trained on her, and smiled.

Pressing her lips together, she bit back a smile of her own. She could control Red, at least a little, by his desire to see her squirm. He would let them look at the files. It was enough for now. And maybe, while she had him distracted by the files, she or Linc could gain the upper hand.

Facing the front again, she remembered the look on Matthew's face earlier in the day when he'd asked if someone else had died. Whatever it took, she had to fight to stay alive. The boys needed her. No. They didn't *need her.* She wasn't mother material. But they needed her to stay alive. It would be too much for their hearts if they lost another family member so soon after their parents died. Adeline could not let that happen.

TWELVE

They had been on the road for an hour and a half and were nearing the point where they'd have to put the address into the GPS navigation. Linc was still unsure how he'd be able to get the upper hand on Red and take all three guns away from him. After the initial exchange between Adeline and Red, silence had fallen over the vehicle, only broken by an occasional outburst of laughter from the back seat and the mumbled words "the shock will kill you," more laughter, and then "save a bullet."

Manic laughter filled the vehicle once again, and Adeline leaned ever so slightly toward Linc. "We're about fifteen minutes away from the point where we need the GPS," she whispered.

"I know." He sighed. If only Red hadn't taken their phones, along with their guns. He or Adeline could have gotten a message to Ryan, and the police could have put up a roadblock or something on one of these back roads where innocent people wouldn't have been at risk of getting killed.

The laughter broke off. "Stop your whispering!" Red growled and sat straighter, looking out the windows. "We left the city long ago. Time to put the address into the GPS."

Linc caught the gunman's eye in the rearview mirror. "Not yet. I still know where we are."

Adeline shrieked. Lincoln glanced in her direction. Red held her by her ponytail. His gun was pressed to the back of her head.

"I said. Turn. It. On. Now!"

"Okay. We'll get directions on the map." Linc fought to keep his voice calm. "But you'll have to let her go. I don't know the address, and I'm not familiar with the navigation system in this vehicle. She'll have to pull it up."

Red released Adeline's ponytail and shoved her head forward. She yelped in pain, jerked the ponytail holder out of her hair and massaged her scalp. The urge to reach out and offer comfort washed over Linc, but instead he tightened his grip on the steering wheel. Too much interaction between them would only make the gunman think there was more to their relationship than boss and employee.

He wasn't an expert in human behavior, but he'd witnessed Sawyer in action enough times to pick up on certain cues. Linc had no doubt if Red thought his feelings for Adeline went deeper than surface level, he'd find even more ways to hurt her to keep Linc in line.

Surface level. Who are you trying to kid? Your feelings go way deeper than that.

No. He tamped down his inner voice. He and Adeline were friends. Nothing more.

She leaned closer to the navigation screen, her long hair falling in a drape, blocking her face from Red's view. "What now?" she whispered.

"Put in the address," Linc answered under his breath, his lips barely moving.

"Move your hair. So I can watch you." Red was becoming more aggressive.

Adeline straightened and started punching buttons on the screen.

Linc turned his full focus back to the road. As he guided the vehicle around a curve, the headlights glinted on something up ahead. An idea sparked. He slowed his speed.

"Hurry," Linc commanded calmly. "Then sit back. We're nearing a big curve in the road, and you're blocking my view."

She glared at him, then pushed the start button and settled back into her seat.

"Starting navigation to 7632 Lakeshore Road," the automated voice stated, loud and clear.

He continued to climb the mountain at a slower pace, the object in the road coming into sight. It was a mangled yellow caution sign. Skid marks indicated some unfortunate driver had lost control on the curve and knocked over the post. The sharp edges of the sign protruded a few inches into the road.

"Why are you going so slow? Speed up!" Red demanded.

"Just trying to be cautious. Figured you'd want to get there in one piece." Linc shrugged and tried to sound nonchalant. "These curves are sharp. There are a lot of skid marks on the road. I'm guessing some drivers underestimate the curves and end up in the ditch."

"Fine. But as soon as we get through them, speed up."

Once Linc knew the front tire was near the sign, he jerked the wheel to the right. "Sorry," he yelled as the tire bounced over the signpost. He had only intended for the metal edge of the sign to puncture the sidewall of the tire, but he'd swerved too far right. Quickly correcting the vehicle, he avoided damaging the back tire, too. With only one spare, he couldn't afford to damage two tires. "Pothole."

"Looks like there was more than one," Red ground out as Linc straightened the vehicle back onto the road. "Don't pull that stunt again, unless you're avoiding a hole that's large enough to swallow the entire vehicle. Got it?"

"Yes." He glanced at Adeline. She gripped the dashboard, but she had a smile on her face. He wondered if she'd seen the metal sign and realized what he'd attempted. Not that it mattered. It seemed the tread on the Jeep's tires had withstood the incident. Linc would have to come up with another plan once they reached the lake house.

They continued the ride in silence. Linc monitored the navigation map. The miles ticked by rapidly. Eighteen miles from where he ran over the caution sign, the low-tire alert beeped and flashed on the vehicle instrument panel.

"What's that? Tell me what's going on!" Red demanded.

"Flat tire," Linc replied.

"You dumb…" Red continued to call him every name he could think of.

"Hey, man. Accidents happen. Especially on dark roads in the middle of the night." He lifted his foot off the accelerator and looked for a smooth place to pull over.

"What are you doing? You're not stopping."

"Look, there's a spare tire on the back of the Jeep. It won't take me long to change it. If we keep going on a punctured tire, we could have a blowout and end up upside down in a ditch." He activated the vehicle's flashers, pulled onto the shoulder of the road and turned to look at the man in the back seat. "Maybe you don't care because you're planning to kill us, anyway. But are you willing to risk your life?"

Red glared at him, a scowl on his face. Linc could almost see the thoughts running through Red's mind as he weighed his words. "Oh, all right! But don't think for one minute that I'll let my guard down. You will change the tire, while I keep the woman by my side…with the gun pressed to her temple and my finger *on* the trigger. One move, accidental or otherwise, and the gun will go off. Got it?"

Linc's throat tightened as fear that one wrong move would cost Addie her life assailed him. *Lord, please guide my steps. Show me an opening so I can put an end to this without putting Adeline's life in danger.* Peace that he could only find in the Lord washed over him and swept his fears away. Meeting their abductor's eyes, he nodded. "Understood."

Red unbuckled his seat belt and leaned forward, pressing the barrel of the gun against Adeline's head for what seemed like the hundredth time. "Fine. Jameson, get out of the vehicle first. Cross to the other side of the road, until I give the okay."

"Go on," Adeline urged, her eyes showing total trust in him. When he hesitated, she added, "I'm fine."

Red fisted a chunk of Addie's hair and held her in place. She winced and clamped her jaws but did not cry out in pain. Linc desperately wished to pull her into his arms and shield her from the gunman, but to do so would result in more torture from their captor.

"Okay. I'm going." He exited the vehicle, crossed the road, then turned around and faced the Jeep with his hands up and palms out. Thankfully, the glow of the full moon overhead illuminated the scene before him enough for him to make out what was happening.

There was an exchange of words between Addie and Red. Linc strained to hear what was being said, to no avail. *Come on, Addie. Follow his directions. Don't pull any heroic stunts until I'm back across the road with the lug wrench in my hand.*

Never taking his eyes off the duo, he watched as Adeline put her hair back into a ponytail. Red exited the vehicle, reached inside, grasped her hair and then dragged her to a boulder about twenty feet from the rear of the Jeep. Addie sat on the rock, with Red standing behind her and the gun pressed against her head. Linc walked slowly back across the road. He had hoped Red would have stood closer to the vehicle to oversee the tire being replaced. He should have known the man was smarter than that.

Looked like it was time for plan B. He'd have to come up with some sort of ruse to get Red to come close enough that he could hit him with the lug wrench. *Lord, I may have to fib to get us out of this situation. Please understand, it's only to catch a killer and to keep Adeline safe.*

Adeline's head throbbed. Red had yanked her hair so many times, she was sure that she had a large bald spot on the crown of her head. She rubbed her temples and reminded herself the situation could be worse. Hair would grow back. Her life would not. As long as Red was pulling her hair, he wasn't pulling the trigger.

Reaching down, she traced circles in the dirt, the fine gravel sticking to her fingers. For a split second, she wondered if she could sling a fistful of the dirt into her captor's eyes and overpower him. But she squelched that idea.

If his weapon discharged, he might hit Linc. She could not take the chance. Maybe later, she would have the opportunity. Fisting a handful of the soil, she folded her hands in her lap.

"I saw that. Put it back. And dust your hands off."

No use pretending she didn't know what he was talking about. She held her hand to the side and let the dirt funnel to the ground. Then she dusted her hands.

"Good girl," he whispered, his breath brushing the nape of her neck.

She clenched her teeth and willed herself to stay perfectly still. Adeline would not allow him to goad her into a response.

"You and your boyfriend would have to be a lot smarter to one-up me. I was a member of the navy elite. I have participated in things that would make you puke. So don't think something as juvenile as throwing dirt in my face would faze me. Got it."

"So, you were a Navy SEAL." She scoffed. "That might impress me if you hadn't frightened innocent children and weren't holding me and *my boss* hostage."

"I couldn't care less what you think of me. I never intended to harm the boys. If Isaac had minded his own business, he and your sister would still be alive. And if you'd taken the boys to live with you after Isaac and Vanessa died, we never would have crossed paths." He yanked harder on her ponytail and tears stung her eyes. "Just be thankful that, after tonight, I'll disappear. After a tragic accident where you and your boss die, of course. And as long as the boys can't identify me, I'll leave them in peace. So go to your grave knowing they'll have a happy life living with your mother in Florida."

Florida. He knew where her parents lived, and where the boys would live after she was gone.

"You'll excuse me if I don't find comfort in that, considering my not being here to raise the boys means my sister's last wish isn't being fulfilled." A jolt of awareness pierced her soul. She needed—no, she wanted—to raise the boys. To be the one who doctored their boo-boos when they got scraped knees playing sports. The one who comforted them when each experienced their first broken heart. The one who taught them to drive then stayed up worrying when they missed curfew. And she would not let this evil man rob her of those experiences. Closing her eyes, she prayed.

Lord, forgive me my lack of faith in the past. I know You are the Light. And only You can overcome the darkness that has engulfed my family. Whatever direction my life takes, whether it ends today or I am around for many, many years for the boys, I pray, Lord, that Your Will be done.

She opened her eyes and focused on Linc as he tightened the lug nuts, glancing over his shoulder toward the boulder at her and Red. He must be looking for an opening to act. No matter what he'd said earlier, she'd known running over the downed caution sign hadn't been an accident. Adeline needed to distract Red so Linc could put whatever plan he had hatched into action. Pushing to her feet, she stood and stretched.

"What are you doing?" Red rounded the boulder.

"Stretching. My back hurts from sitting." She lifted her arms above her head and stretched from one side to the other. Out of the corner of her eye, she watched Linc slide the lug wrench in front of the Jeep.

"Then you need to tell your boyfriend…I mean *boss*… to hurry," he sneered and shifted his stance, making it easier for him to keep her and Linc both in his sight.

Linc quickly lifted the damaged tire, carried it to the back of the Jeep, dropped it inside and slammed the cargo door.

"Okay. All done." He turned, wiped his hands on his jeans and took a step in their direction.

"Don't come any closer," Red ordered. "Go stand in front of the vehicle. Keep your hands up."

Linc walked backward to the front of the Jeep, his hands in clear view, and paused only inches from where she'd seen him put the lug wrench. If Red followed the same pattern he had back at the house, he'd have her get into the vehicle first, then he'd get in behind her. If Linc timed it just right, would he be able to grab the lug wrench and deliver a blow before Red could react?

Red stayed a few steps behind her, for once allowing her to walk without being dragged by her hair. If she created a diversion, Linc might have a better chance of delivering a blow with the wrench.

Adeline came even with the back door of the Jeep, met Linc's gaze and winked. *Please, Lord, let him realize what I'm doing and react quickly.* She pretended to stumble and fell forward, landing on her hands and knees.

"Get up!" Red yelled and reached for her.

Before he could grab hold of her, Adeline pushed off with her hands, planted her feet below her in a deep squat and sprang upward. Then in one swift move, she spun and flung dirt into his eyes. The gun discharged and the bullet hit the ground inches from her feet.

"Duck!" Linc yelled.

She dropped to the ground as he swung the lug wrench above her head. He hit Red across the forearm and knocked the weapon out of his hand, sending it into the weeds. Red reached behind his back, trying to get his hands on the guns he'd taken from her and Linc earlier. Linc pulled her to her feet, pushed her behind him, and swung the wrench repeatedly, forcing the gunman to continue dodging the iron tool and keeping him from grasping one of the weapons. Linc swung again. Red grabbed the end of the wrench, and what ensued was a harrowing game of tug-of-war.

The gun! She needed to find Red's gun. Adeline dove into the weeds and frantically patted the ground, searching. She ignored the briars and gravel biting into her palms. Her hand brushed the cold steel barrel. She palmed the weapon and raised to her feet. The lug wrench lay on the ground near the Jeep. Linc and Red were locked in hand-to-hand combat near the edge of the shoulder that separated the road from a deep ditch. Raising the weapon in her hand, Adeline fired a shot into an elm tree. Both men froze and looked in her direction, Linc partially blocking Red from her view. Red reached back then raised his arm, moonlight glinting on a gun.

"Look out!" Adeline yelled.

Linc executed a high roundhouse kick to Red's chest. The gun flew out of his hand and skittered into the road. Red stumbled backward, lost his footing and tumbled down the slope into the ditch.

She dashed into the road and picked up the gun—the one Red had taken from her—then raced back to Linc, who stood on the edge of the ditch. "I have both guns. Where'd he go?"

"After landing at the bottom, he ran up the other side

and into the woods." He puffed out a breath and pushed his hand through his hair.

"Should we go after him?" She took a step forward, but Linc put a hand on her arm, halting her.

"No. We can't afford to waste time searching in the dark. The best thing to do is get to the lake house before him and find the documents."

"Do you think he'll make it that far on foot? We're still about twenty miles away."

"I heard him tell you he was a former SEAL. They're taught to never give up, even in the most difficult circumstances. Besides, my grandmother used to say 'a bad penny always turns up.' I think Isaac named his former partner Copper because he knew the man was like that bad penny and would keep showing up and putting his family in danger, even after Isaac was gone. I have no doubt Copper, Red or whatever you want to call him, will make it to the lake house. We just have to get there before him. But first…" He grasped her shoulders and pulled her into a warm embrace.

She should pull away. Instead, she wrapped her arms around his waist and laid her head against his chest. For the first time since Red had grabbed her, she felt safe. And though she realized this sense of security would be short-lived once Red showed back up, she wouldn't give in to that fear. For now, she would absorb the warmth of the embrace, letting it recharge her.

All too soon, Linc kissed the top of her head and pulled away. "Let's go."

They raced to the Jeep, settling into the same seats they'd vacated earlier. Typically, Adeline would insist on driving since it was her vehicle, but she needed to focus her energy on figuring out other clues Isaac had left behind. Once they got to the lake house, every minute would count. Because it didn't matter what Red had said. Without a doubt, if she lost her life tonight, the twins never would be safe. All of their lives were on the line, which meant she was the one walking the tightrope and trying to get to the other side of this horrible situation Isaac had left behind.

THIRTEEN

"In nine hundred feet, your destination is on the right," the automated GPS voice said.

Linc eased off the accelerator and slowed, searching for the driveway.

"There!" Adeline exclaimed, pointing in the distance. "The drive is on the other side of that stone-column mailbox. The drive is long and winds through the trees then it opens in the clearing and you'll see the house. We'll start there. Though I have no clue where to look."

"It's okay. We will figure it out. Together." He reached across and squeezed her hand. Linc didn't know why he needed to touch her. Was it because he had come so close to losing her? If the shot hadn't gone wild earlier, it would have killed her. No. That might be part of it, but he also knew if it had been any other employee with their life on the line, he would not have embraced them, nor would he be holding their hand now.

Linc dropped her hand and activated the blinker, turning onto the drive that he hoped would lead them to answers. His smartwatch rang, breaking the silence, and he gasped. Ryan's name flashed on the tiny display screen. How could Linc have forgotten? When he upgraded his watch last month, he'd purchased the one with cellular capability, at Ryan's insistence. He pressed the phone button and draped his arm across the steering wheel. "Hi, Ryan."

"You never called me back. Did you make it to the lake house yet?"

"We ran into a little trouble." Linc pulled to a stop in front of the lake house—a moderate-size, single-story log home—and quickly filled his partner in on the events that had transpired since he'd sent the text to let Ryan know they were headed to Lake Granby. "I should have called you after we ditched Red, but I forgot my watch had cellular service, until you called. Can you call the Grand County Sheriff's Office and ask them to be on the lookout for Red? Tell them he's wanted for questioning in Denver in connection to a break-in and a drive-by shooting. Tell them you had a tip he was in the area and on foot. Don't let them know we're here, though. We don't need them showing up, slowing us down in our search, because that would just give Red more time to get here before we find the documents."

"Okay. But if Red shows up there, call for backup." Silence came across the line as Ryan waited for his agreement.

He appreciated his friend's concern, but Linc didn't need reminding how dangerous Red was. If he showed up, Linc would immediately dial nine-one-one. He would not take a chance with Addie's life again.

"Linc. You still there?"

"Yeah. I'm here. And I hear you. I'll call the sheriff if Red shows up here. Keep the boys safe. We have a treasure hunt to finish. I'll call you as soon as we head back to Denver." Linc disconnected the call and met Addie's gaze. "Are you ready?"

"More than ready. Let's go." She slipped her gun out of her holster and exited the vehicle.

He palmed Red's gun, thankful to have a weapon for self-defense if there was trouble. But also regretful that he'd let the thug steal his Glock. He would have to go to the police station in the morning and report it stolen. Puffing out a breath, he joined Adeline on the porch.

"There's no obvious sign Red beat us here, but I'd feel better if we clear the house room by room before we start our search."

He nodded agreement. "Sounds good. Do you remember if there's an alarm system here?"

"Yes. It's just like the one at the house. I mean the old one." She pulled the key out of her pocket. "I'm pretty sure the code is the same, so it should be easy to disarm."

They entered the house and she disarmed the alarm before it alerted the security company to their presence. Then they cleared the house—three bedrooms, two bathrooms, living room, eat-in kitchen, game room and two-car garage.

"All clear." He holstered the weapon. "Where do you want to begin?"

After securing her own gun, she pulled a hair tie out of her pocket and gathered her long brown hair into a ponytail. "Master bedroom, I guess."

Ninety minutes later, they had searched the entire house, beginning in the master bedroom then working their way through the remaining rooms and ending in the garage. There were no filing cabinets or hidden safes anywhere to be found.

"Should we search the attic?" Linc pointed to the pull-cord that dangled from the ceiling in the garage.

"I went up there last summer with Vanessa. The only things up there are a few old windows and some of the twins' old toys—like a rocking horse and some of those big metal dump trucks—Vanessa wanted to keep for future grandchildren. Nothing else. No boxes or anything." A strand of hair had broken free from Addie's ponytail and fallen across her face. She puffed out a breath and blew it out of her eyes. "Let's search the boathouse first. If it isn't there, then we can search the attic."

He swept his arm toward the door into the house. "Lead the way. But remember to stay on high alert while we're outdoors. If Red found someone willing to give him a ride, it's possible he'll show up soon."

She palmed her gun as they made their way through the kitchen and out the double French doors. "Oh, believe me, I will not give him another chance to get the jump on me. Once was enough."

For me, too. He hoped never to experience the helpless sensation of seeing her with a gun pointed at her head ever again. On high alert, Linc followed close behind her, scanning the property in front, behind and on both sides of them. The inky-black night had shifted to a hazy gray color in preparation of the sunrise that would peek on the horizon in about thirty minutes. He could see farther, but not far enough that he could make out the dark shadows of the woods. Red had the perfect place to hide and watch.

An icy shiver ran up his spine and goose bumps popped out on his arms. He'd never been one to frighten easily, but he wanted to race to the safety of the boathouse sitting fifty yards away. Picking up his pace, he urged Addie along. "Let's hurry. We're easy targets out here in the open."

She nodded, and they sprinted the remaining distance.

They reached the dock. Addie pulled out Vanessa's key ring and fumbled through the keys until she found the one she was looking for. Closing her fingers around it, she grabbed hold of the doorknob and the door popped open before she inserted the key into the lock. She looked up, her eyes wide.

Linc motioned for her to get behind him. "Where's the light switch?" he asked, his voice barely above a whisper.

She put a hand on his back. "On the left side of the door frame."

"I'll go left. You go right." He reached his left hand inside and found the light switch plate. "There are four switches. Which one is for the inside light?"

"The first one. I think," came the whispered reply.

He hoped she was right. They would only have one chance at getting the jump on Red if he were inside. "Okay. On three. One…two…three."

Linc swiped his hand upward, pushed the door wide and darted inside. He stopped short and blinked several times, desperate to get his bearings. The entire building was flooded in light so bright it felt almost like being back on his high school football field on a Friday night. If Red were hiding in the woods nearby and not inside the building, Linc had just shone a beacon on their location and made them easy targets.

Realizing what had happened, Adeline quickly switched off the overhead fluorescent lights and switched on the lower-wattage lights. "Sorry," she whispered, though she doubted if there was much point in trying to avoid detection now. "It was the second one."

"Why would anyone install lights like that in such a small space?"

"Isaac said they made it easier for him to see when he was working on the boat." She shrugged, trying to erase her feeling of incompetence as much as anything. How could she make such a careless mistake?

"I doubt Red is in here, or he would have jumped out already and gained the upper hand. But we still need to check." She took two steps into the boathouse and froze. "The boat's gone!"

"I'm sure it's being stored in dry dock for the winter. It's too cold on this lake to leave it in a boathouse year-round." He eyed the hydraulic lift system that flanked the ten-foot by twenty-six-foot boat slip in the center of the building. "Even with the ability to lift the boat out of the water for winter, the cold would be too much and cost thousands of dollars' worth of damage to the watercraft."

The inside of the boathouse was roughly seven hundred square feet and consisted of a six-foot-wide, U-shaped wooden dock that bordered the front and side walls, and a metal garage style door on the back wall that allowed the boat to enter and exit. Without the twenty-four-foot boat in the center of the building, the space looked bare. A tall tool cabinet stood in one corner, beside a workbench and a stool. Two paddles hung on one wall and an eighteen-foot canoe hung from the rafters.

Warring emotions bubbled up inside Adeline. On the one hand, she was relieved there were no places where Red could hide, but on the other, the missing boat and lack of hiding spaces also meant the documents they were looking for probably weren't in the boathouse.

If Red didn't break into the boathouse, then why had the

door opened when she touched it? Adeline turned to the door, grasped the knob and twisted. "It's locked. Maybe the latch didn't catch the last time it was closed and that's why it popped open."

"If that were the case, wouldn't the wind from one of the winter storms have blown it open before now?" Linc brushed past her.

She followed him onto the dock and listened. The early morning was eerily quiet. The sound of the waves gently bushing against the dock. "I'd like to search the tool chest before we leave. It's the only place we haven't checked for the documents."

Linc nodded. "Okay. You search. I'll stand guard."

Adeline reentered the boathouse and crossed to the opposite wall where the tall, red metal cabinet stood. She opened the top drawer. The latch was broken. "Um… Linc. Red's been here. The tool chest lock has been pried open." She looked in the second and third drawers, panic rising inside her. "All the drawers are empty."

Adeline met Linc's gaze as he stood in the doorway, peering inside. "What did he do with the tools?" she asked.

"The water," they said in unison.

Rushing to the edge of the boat dock, she peered into the icy blue, gray water. She couldn't see anything. If the tools were at the bottom of the lake, there wasn't anything she could do about it.

Adeline straightened and turned to leave. Red jumped from the top of the boathouse onto the pier with a resounding thud. As if she were watching an instant replay, the scene before her played out in slow motion. Linc turned toward the sound. Red rammed into him mid-turn. Linc flew backward on the interior dock, his upper body falling over the edge of the boat slip, toward the icy waters. He grabbed a cleat—a T-shaped metal device bolted to the dock for tying a rope and securing a boat—with his right hand, straining to hold his body out of the water.

"I warned you things wouldn't end well for you." Red's manic laughter rang out. He slammed the boathouse door shut, and hammering sounds ensued.

Addie braced herself against one of the metal columns spaced eight feet apart on both sides of the dock and extended a hand to Linc.

Sweat beaded his hairline. His white knuckled hand clung to the cleat and his upper body shook as he fought to keep his torso inches above the water. He couldn't hold on much longer. It was only a matter of time before he plunged into the freezing waters below.

"Reach with your free hand," she ordered.

The muscles on his right arm tightened and, with a grunt, he pulled his upper body a few inches higher. His fingers brushed the tips of hers. Almost there. She stretched as far as she dared, grasped his left hand and tugged. They fell side by side onto the dock, gasping for air.

"Red...locked...us in," Adeline panted.

Linc pushed to his feet and rushed to the door. He rammed his shoulder against it, but to no avail. "It won't budge."

"I think he nailed it shut." Adeline looked for another exit. "Why aren't there any windows in here?"

Linc sighed. "Maybe the builder didn't feel the need to install them since this isn't living space." He shoved a hand through his hair. "I can't believe I let Red get the jump on me, again."

"It's my fault. I didn't even think about the rooftop

deck. The stairs leading to it are on the other side of the building. I was too focused on searching for the documents." The feeling of being a sitting target waiting for Red to make his next move rattled her nerves. "You know, he's got to be planning something. He wouldn't just leave us in here alive. We're too much of a risk. He can't chance we'll get out."

"Yeah. I know. I'll call the sheriff—" Linc lifted his arm. It was bare. His smartwatch must have fallen into the lake. He scrubbed a hand over his face. "Okay, new plan. Check every corner of this building and see if you can find any kind of waterproof dry bag big enough to hold my weapon."

"What are you planning?"

"The only way out is in the water. I'll swim out and open the door from the outside."

"That's too dangerous. You'll be risking hypothermia."

"Look, Addie, I'm not waiting around for him to come back and kill us. I'll be fine. Some people believe swimming in extreme cold water is good for your health."

She pointed up to the rafters. "But we have a canoe."

He looked up then scanned the open space. "I don't see a ladder. Or a pulley system. How do you propose we get it down?"

"My brother-in-law liked gadgets. He was also a brilliant engineer." She turned to the keypad mounted to the right of the light switches and punched in the code. A soft whirling nose sounded as the small motor hidden in the rafters lowered the canoe until it was a couple of feet above the platform.

"Well, that's handy." Linc crossed to the canoe. "Let's get this down. We'll put it in the water, and then you can raise the garage door. It's likely to be louder, which will alert Red to our escape and make him come running."

She pulled the paddles off the wall and tossed them into the small boat. "Why do you think he didn't just come in and shoot us earlier?"

"We have guns. He may have taken out one of us, but the one he didn't get would take him out."

"So, he's going to wait until we escape and take us out?"

Linc pinned her with his gaze. "I don't know what he's thinking. But once we're in the water, I'll paddle and you keep your gun handy and stay on lookout."

The lump in her throat prevented a verbal response, so she nodded. In the past two-years, she'd witnessed Linc's take-charge attitude. His constant need to take on the toughest jobs. And the weight of the responsibilities he carried on his shoulders. She was ashamed to admit, even to herself, that she'd thought his *take-charge attitude* was all about control. Now she knew better. Being a protector, putting himself in danger before others, came naturally to him. Addie knew he'd prefer to be the one on lookout. But his trust in her ability to take out Red, if it came down to it, would not be misplaced.

She crinkled her nose. "Do you smell smoke?"

Thick, gray smoke billowed into the space. Flames hungrily ate through the bottom of the wooden walls on three sides.

"It's spreading fast! He must've used an accelerant," Link exclaimed. "Open the garage door!"

Adeline raced to the keypad and quickly punched in the code. Then she rushed back to Linc. The metal garage door inched upward as they lowered the canoe into the icy water. He held the boat steady while she climbed in and settled into the bow, and then he took his position in the stern. Using their hands, they pushed off from the dock. There was an explosion, sparks rained behind them and the power went out. The garage door stopped only one-third of the way up.

Linc paddled the canoe down the center of the boat slip, maneuvering around chunks of ice. "Get in the bottom of the boat!"

She eased backward out of the cane seat and laid down in the canoe. Linc joined her as the small boat slid under the garage door and out into the open lake. "Let me get settled in my seat so I can stabilize the canoe before you move, okay?"

"Yes," she whispered, her breath forming puffs of fog. The temperature felt like it had dropped ten degrees or more out on the windy, icy lake.

The canoe cut through the water as Linc executed long strokes with the oars. "Okay, you can get up now, but be cautious. I'd prefer not taking an icy dip in the lake if possible."

"Don't worry. I have no intention of flipping us." She moved with thoughtful, snail-like movements, releasing a sigh of relief after she settled back onto her seat.

Sunrise was in full bloom, streaks of orange, yellow, red and purple painting the sky. The beauty of God's artwork was all around them, but evil lurked in the shadows.

Lord, please, let us capture Red and make it back to the boys.

"I'll head to that outcropping of pine trees, so we're not out in the open." Linc pointed with an oar. "Turn around and watch behind me. Don't let Red surprise us. Find him before he finds us."

She did as he instructed, then palmed her weapon and scanned the shoreline. Lights were coming on inside the homes that scattered the shoreline. People were waking to greet the day.

Fire fully engulfed the boathouse. The smoke plume reached high into the sky. It wouldn't be long before it attracted attention from nearby residents. Help surely would be on the way soon.

A dark shadow raced from the back of the lake house and down to the shoreline, running parallel with them.

"He's on the shore!" She watched Red lift his arm and aim.

The sound of shots fired rang out in the early morning stillness. Either Red was unaware of how close the other houses along the shore were because of the isolated feeling the developer had created with the trees around each property, or he had ceased to care and was willing to take out any neighbor who might get in the way.

Linc dug deep into the icy water with his paddle, urging the canoe forward as he alternated from one side to the other. Addie would never get a clear shot from this distance, so she slipped the gun back into its holster, grabbed the other oar from the floor of the boat, flipped her legs to the front of the bow and mimicked his strokes.

"What are you doing?"

"Helping," she yelled over her shoulder.

The spring thaw had reached the area a little early this year, but ice still covered much of the lake. Working together, they navigated the small streams of water that flowed between the ice chunks. They maneuvered around the outcropping of trees, blocking Red's view of them and, Addie hoped, slowing him down on his attempt to reach them.

"Okay, put your paddle back into the boat, and take up your guard post again," Linc instructed. "I'll get us to that dock over there, then we'll circle back on foot and intercept him."

Addie lifted her paddle out of the water, turned and slid it back onto the floor of the canoe, catching the determined look on Linc's face. He reminded her of Dylan, the last man who'd been so fiercely protective of her and others and had lost his life trying to protect and serve.

Thank You, Lord, for this man and his determination to protect me and the twins. Please keep him safe from harm.

If anything happened to Linc while he was trying to protect her, she didn't know if she'd survive the heartache. Realization struck like a bolt of lightning. Somewhere along the line, he'd switched from being just her boss to being someone she cared deeply for.

Once this ordeal was over, she would have to decide if she could continue to work for Protective Instincts or if she needed to move on to something else. Maybe she could find a job in Florida and she and her nephews could get a home near her parents. Having family close by to help when needed would be nice. It seemed not only her feelings for Linc had changed, but she'd also had a change of heart about being a mom.

FOURTEEN

Linc caught movement out of the corner of his eye. A shadow wove between the trees on the shoreline. He drove the oar deep into the water and pulled back. Nice, even, forward strokes, the bow of the canoe zeroing in on the dock that ran the length of the left side of a boathouse like an arrow aiming for the gold center of an archery target.

His shoulders burned from the exertion. Silently chanting marching cadences in his head, he maintained a steady rhythm. Almost there.

The front of the bow came even with the dock and Adeline reached out, grasped hold of the side and pulled the canoe close. She hopped out, laid on her stomach and held the boat in place. He climbed onto the dock and together they hoisted the canoe out of the water and turned it upside down on the dock. Then they raced to the shore, their feet pounding on the wooden boards.

"Hey, what are you doing there?" a male voice yelled from the screened porch of a house forty yards away.

"There's a shooter! Call nine-one-one and lock yourself inside your house." Linc palmed the weapon he carried and flattened his back against the boathouse, motioning for Addie to get beside him.

The man who appeared to be in his sixties, scurried indoors and slammed the door.

"You think he'll tell the police about the shooter, or just report us?" she asked, breathing heavily.

"I don't know." He puffed out a breath. There would be a lot of explaining to do once the police arrived, and a chance he and Addie would be mistaken for the bad guys. "We can't worry about that too much at the moment."

"What's the plan?"

He pointed to a large pine tree ten feet away. "Run to that tree, as fast as you can. Then work your way up the bank, going from tree to tree. Once you get high enough that you have a clear view, run back to your sister's lake house. Meet the first responders when they show up and alert them to the situation. We don't want any of them getting shot by Red. Got it?"

She nodded. "What are you going to do?"

"I'll stick closer to the shoreline and then angle upward about twenty feet as I near the woods. Red seemed to struggle, working his way through the underbrush, which is probably thickest near the water. If I can get to a point where the woods aren't as thick, I should be able to circle around behind him and get the jump on him—and, I hope, subdue him before he kills someone."

Concern etched Addie's face, evidence of an argument brewing in her mind. He knew she'd prefer sticking together, and ideally, he would, too. "The last thing we need is the first responders coming on scene unaware of the situation unfolding. We want them to know we're the good guys, so they don't accidentally shoot one of us."

Her face shuttered. "Don't get shot," she said tersely and darted to the tree.

He watched briefly as she ran from tree to tree, making her way up the sloped yard. Her acquiescence stunned him. Once this was over, he'd want to know what put that look of intense pain in her eyes. With no time to worry about what he'd said to cause such a response, Linc stooped low and raced along the shoreline. His eyes fixed on the woods as he searched for movement. Where had Red gone?

Stopping behind a small shed at the edge of the property, he inhaled and exhaled a few steady breaths. The sun inched upward and, despite the near-freezing temperature, sweat beaded his forehead.

He was momentarily transported back to his first military deployment overseas, tracking enemy soldiers through unknown terrain. Two of his military brothers had lost their lives during that mission. It had been Linc's first experience dealing with the death of friends, men his age robbed of living a full life. He'd had to learn to compartmentalize each experience and not let it cripple him and his ability to do his job. Linc had to execute his plan flawlessly or his life would be the one cut short, and he wouldn't be around to protect Addie or the twins.

An image of Addie looking out the window watching him and the boys playing in the backyard after dinner last night came to mind. Despite the danger that stalked them, in the last twenty-four hours, there had been fleeting moments of happiness and laughter. Feeding the giraffes at the zoo. Playing fetch with Gunther. Watching the boys act out their father's bedtime story. Realization dawned on Linc that he wanted to experience more moments like that. The twins would need a male influence in their lives, and he wanted it to be him. But he didn't just want to be in the twins' lives. He wanted to be the man in Adeline's life, too. However, they'd have to get out of this situation alive before they could discuss the possibility of that happening. Even if he and Addie couldn't have a relationship, he would always be there for her and the boys.

He exhaled a breath and peered around the building. There was a rustling sound in the woods. Hard to tell if it was a wild animal or Red. A twig snapped behind him, and he swung around, his gun raised.

"Don't shoot," the man from the deck demanded in a hushed voice, coming toward him dressed in camo, a rifle at his side.

"What are you doing? I told you to stay inside." The last thing Linc needed was for the neighbor to be put in harm's way.

"I have every right to be out here. It's my property." The man, with short-cropped gray hair and a muscular build, plastered his back to the shed and pinned Linc with his gaze. "Retired Major Harry Montgomery, US Army Special Forces. Not to brag, but I'm one of the best snipers the military ever trained. Now, tell me what the situation is here."

"Lincoln Jameson. Owner of Protective Instincts— a security protection firm in Denver. The female is one of my employees. Someone killed her sister and brother-in-law, and two days after their funeral, a man named Red—six feet tall, muscular build, red hair—broke into the family home looking for something the brother-in-law left behind. My employee was there with her two young nephews during the break-in. Now Red is trying to kill us."

"He the one that started that fire?" Harry asked, sniffing the air.

"Yes. It's the boathouse. He locked us inside, but we escaped in the canoe."

"What's he after?"

Linc liked Harry Montgomery. He asked direct questions and got to the core of the matter. "He's a former Navy SEAL. We believe my employee's brother-in-law, who was a former navy engineer, had evidence Red was selling top-secret military information."

"Where'd Adeline go?"

"She went—wait…you know her?"

"No. But I knew Isaac and Vanessa. Fine folks. I heard what happened to them and expected Vanessa's sister to show up eventually. Just not like this."

Linc processed the information. He wondered what Harry meant about expecting Addie to show up, but his curiosity about that subject would have to wait. First, they had to capture Red. "I sent Addie back to the house to meet the first responders. I didn't want them to come on scene without knowing what was going on. Trying to avoid accidents."

"Smart thinking. Don't want them to shoot you instead of Red. I had the same thought. That's why, when I called in the report of a shooter, I gave them a rough description of you and Adeline—gender, clothes, approximate height—and told them you were the ones being shot at." Harry lifted his rifle and pointed it upward. "If you're ready. I've got—"

A female scream pierced the air.

"Addie!" Linc took off in the direction the sound had come from, Harry at his heels.

"We need to fan out. He's expecting you, but he's not expecting me."

"I'll go high. You go low," Linc barked.

Harry reached out a hand and halted him. "Remember. I'm a trained sniper. A good one. Don't make any sudden moves that will put you between me and Red. Got it?"

Linc pressed his lips together, nodded and took off again in the direction of the scream. He appreciated the older man's desire to be helpful, but if Red had harmed Addie, Linc wouldn't need any help taking him out.

Adeline's ankle burned and sharp pains radiated up her leg. She'd broken her ankle when she'd tripped over the log. If the sound of the snap when she'd fallen hadn't convinced her, the pain and inability to put weight on her foot did.

She needed to find a place to hide. Her involuntary scream of pain when she'd tumbled probably had alerted Red to her whereabouts. And she'd lost her weapon in the fall. How could she have been so careless? She scooted up against the log and pulled as much dirt, twigs and leaves over her as she could. Adeline couldn't hide completely, but hoped her dark brown winter coat and cargo pants would blend with the dirt so the small amount of camouflage would be enough to conceal her.

The sound of footsteps pounding through the winter carpet of dried leaves and twigs echoed in the woods. Adeline silently berated herself for her clumsiness.

"Come out, come out, wherever you are." Manic laughter resonated in the early morning silence.

She peeked over the log, careful not to move a muscle. Red walked past her, then stopped and stood not more than three feet from her hiding spot. *I let him get too close.* Dark shadows shrouded Red's face, but she didn't need to see the look in his eyes to know that if he got his hands on her this time, she wouldn't survive.

An excruciating shock of pain shot up her leg, and she bit the inside of her cheek to hold back the scream that crept up her throat. How was she going to evade detection? *Think, Addie. Think!*

Slowly exhaling a silent breath, she willed her nerves to settle. *Dear Heavenly Father, help me. Please, don't let me die like this.*

"Hold it right there, Red! Put down your weapon. It's over." Linc's voice rang out from somewhere to the left of her.

Don't move. Don't move. Don't move. She willed herself to stay frozen in place.

"I don't think so." Red raised his weapon, turned and faced the direction of Linc's voice, and sidestepped closer to the log. His eyes focused straight ahead, he bent down and, with his left hand, yanked her to her feet and pulled her in front of his body.

She cried out in pain as tears stung the backs of her eyes.

"Ah, did you hurt your leg?" Red whispered against her ear, the cold metal of his gun barrel caressing her cheek.

Adeline clinched her teeth and focused on her breathing. She would not allow his goading to rile her.

"Looks like your employee has been injured, Lincoln." Red turned, keeping her in place as a shield. "Should I shoot her and put her out of her misery? That would be the most humane thing to do, right?"

"You do... And. I. Will. Kill. You," Linc said through gritted teeth.

A shiver went up her spine. Linc meant his words. But

with the gun pressed against her temple, they were both helpless to stop Red. She would be dead before Linc could execute a single shot. Adeline had to do something. "Take care of the boys. Tell them I love them."

"Isn't that sweet? Such a doting aunt." Red caressed her cheek with the barrel of the gun as he had earlier.

Biting her lip, she bent her knees slightly and pushed off with her feet. Her head connected with Red's nose. He loosened his hold on her. A fiery hot pain shot through her body. Nausea welled inside her as she fell to the ground and clasped her ankle.

"Why you—" Red pointed his gun at Adeline, anger radiating off him.

A gunshot rang out before Linc could pull his own trigger. A red stain appeared on the right shoulder of Red's sheepskin coat. His weapon fell to the ground, and a look of shock registered on his face as he crumpled to the dirt at Addie's feet.

Linc raced to Addie and sank to the ground beside her. He brushed the hair out of her face and searched her brown eyes. "Are you okay?"

"I broke my ankle," she murmured.

He pulled her into his arms. "Sweetheart, an ankle will heal. I'm just thankful he didn't shoot you."

Harry made his way to them, his gun still trained on Red. "Is she okay?"

"Yes." Linc stood, swooped Addie into his arms, and turned to look at Red, who lay writhing on the ground. "What about him?"

"Eh. He'll survive." Harry kicked Red's gun to the side. "I purposefully shot to injure and not kill. I figured the authorities would prefer him alive. Him being a traitor and all."

Linc nodded. Though he would have preferred to be the one who had saved Addie, he would have shot to kill, not just maim. And Harry was right, Red needed to be alive to stand trial and face the consequences of his actions.

"Who…are you?" Adeline asked, staring at Harry.

"Harry Montgomery, ma'am."

"The man from the porch earlier," Linc attested. "I'll fill you in later."

Addie's lips formed an *O* and she nodded. "Thank you for your help."

"Glad to be of service." He reached down and hauled Red to his feet. "Come on. Let's turn him over to the sheriff."

Red protested and complained, but Harry held firm and forced him along the narrow trail.

Adeline laid her head on Linc's chest. "Thank you. For coming to my rescue. And for carrying me. I'd insist on walking, but—"

"Absolutely not. I saw the pain on your face when Red pulled you to your feet." He tightened his hold. "Want to tell me how you broke your ankle?"

"Carelessness. Plain and simple." She sighed. "I stepped into a shallow hole and tried to recover but ended up tripping over a log. Probably should be glad no one was around with a video camera. I'm sure it looked like a slapstick comedy skit."

He smiled. "Since there's no video evidence, maybe the boys and I can coax you into acting it out for us…once you've healed, of course."

"Not a chance. I need to retain a small amount of dignity."

The laughter that had threatened earlier bubbled over.

Sirens wailed as the first responders drew closer to the lake house. Linc and Adeline emerged from the woods as two firetrucks and a sheriff's deputy cruiser pulled into the drive.

"That's Deputy Harkins. I'll take this guy over to him and explain what happened." Harry dipped his head to Adeline. "Take her indoors and put some ice on that foot. I'll have Harkins call for an ambulance."

"Shouldn't we wait here until the deputy questions us?" Addie asked.

"You can, if you want, but I think you need to get inside and let Linc take that shoe off before you have to be cut out of it." He looked pointedly at her foot.

Linc gasped. Adeline's foot had doubled in size, and the small amount of skin exposed above the sock had turned a nasty red with streaks of dark purplish blue. "Harry's right. I'll deal with the deputy and answer his questions after I get ice on your foot."

The sheriff's deputy pulled to a stop in front of the house, and the tanker fire truck wound its way around the house and as close to the lake's edge as possible, the ladder truck close behind. Harry half dragged a protesting Red toward the deputy, who had exited his vehicle and headed in their direction.

Linc pushed through the double French doors they'd exited earlier and made his way into the kitchen. Once there, he sat Addie on top of the granite countertop, turning her so her foot rested on the counter.

"Get me down. Put me in a chair," she protested.

"Your foot needs to be elevated. This is the easiest way." He untied her shoe and loosened the strings as much as he could. "This is probably going to hurt. I'm sorry."

Grasping the heel, he pulled the shoe off in one swift move. Addie's sharp intake of breath verified his declaration that the movement would be painful.

Time for ice. He searched the cabinet drawers until he found a dish towel. Then he crossed over to the refrigerator and pressed the through-the-door ice dispenser, catching the ice cubes in the towel.

Once he had enough ice, he folded the cloth and tied it around her ankle. Then he took her hand and placed it on top of the towel of ice. "Hold it in place."

Linc wrapped an arm around her shoulders and slid his other arm under her knees. He picked her up and carried her to the sofa, settling her down gently. Grabbing throw pillows from a nearby armchair, he tucked them under the injured foot. Then he raced down the hall to the closest bedroom, snatched a pillow off the bed, and returned to the living room to place the pillow behind her head. "Do you need anything else? Want me to rummage around and see if I can find some pain reliever?"

"No. I'm fine. I read an article once that said when pain levels reach a certain point, your brain blocks the pain so you don't feel it. I think I've reached that point. Either that or the swelling is numbing my foot. Either way, the pain is bearable." She caught his hand and pulled him down to sit on the edge of the sofa. "Thank you for reaching me so quickly and for saving me from Red."

The thought that he'd been so close to losing her overwhelmed him. If he hadn't gotten to her in time… If Adeline hadn't headbutted Red… If Harry hadn't been a trained sniper… If… He released a breath. If things had turned out differently, the nightmares and post-traumatic stress he would have suffered would have been ten times worse than anything he'd ever been through before.

He had experienced a lot of loss in his thirty-seven years—grandparents, numerous military buddies, his sister, whom he'd adored—but somewhere deep inside his soul, he knew the loss of this woman's life would have hurt more than any previous loss had. She was the most beautiful and most courageous woman he'd ever met. Linc had put off facing the reality as long as he could. He couldn't fight it any longer. *He loved her.* But he couldn't tell her that. Not yet. For now, she needed time to heal, emotionally and physically.

"We'll get you to the hospital as soon as we can, and they'll fix you right up." Reaching out, he caressed her cheek with his free hand and leaned forward.

"Linc and Adeline, this is Deputy Harkins. He has some questions for you," Harry declared, entering the room with the deputy close behind.

Embarrassed he'd almost kissed Addie, Linc dropped his hand, jumped to his feet and turned to greet the deputy. Praying he didn't look as flustered as he felt.

Dear Lord, she has been through too much trauma in the past week. She's still figuring out how to navigate her new responsibilities. I can't add to her stress. Help me be patient. To give her time to accept me into her and the twins' lives. And, Lord, if friendship is all we can ever have, help me accept it with gratitude.

FIFTEEN

Adeline's head pounded. She'd been in the ER for four hours and was desperate to go home to see Matthew and Josiah. Of course, the staff in the ER had to prioritize the patients according to the level of trauma, and a broken ankle couldn't take priority over someone who was in cardiac arrest or some other life-or-death situation.

She'd finally had X-rays, and they had confirmed that she had indeed broken her ankle. Fortunately, the break appeared to be one that would mend over time without the need for surgery. The doctor stabilized her ankle with an air cast and told her she'd have to follow up with an orthopedic specialist to get a fiberglass cast. In the meantime, she'd been instructed to stay off her foot, which was a given since any amount of weight on the injured ankle sent red-hot pains shooting up her leg.

The doctor had left her small ER cubicle ten minutes ago, telling her he'd send the nurse in with pain meds and her discharge papers. As eager as she was to see the nurse return with the promised pain relief and the required forms for her release, she was even more anxious for Linc to return.

He'd excused himself to go outside and make some

phone calls when the attendant had arrived to take her for X-rays. An hour later, Linc still hadn't returned. What was taking him so long? Had Red escaped custody? Or had something happened to the twins? If Linc didn't hurry back soon, her imagination would run away with her.

The nurse who had assisted the doctor earlier entered the room with papers tucked under her arm and a tray in her hand, which she extended to Adeline. "Okay, sweetie, swallow these and you'll soon feel better."

Grasping the small paper medicine cup, she tipped the two large pills into the back of her mouth, picked up the cup of water and rinsed them down. "Thank you."

"I have your release forms." The nurse started going through the stack of papers, handing them to Adeline one by one. "This has the details of your appointment with the orthopedic doctor in Denver. We were able to get you in to see him early tomorrow morning. Here's your prescription for the pain meds. The medicine is likely to make you drowsy. Do you have someone to drive you home and stay with you for the next few days?"

"Her mother is visiting," Linc answered as he walked into the room. "And I'll also check in daily."

"Oh, good." The nurse handed Adeline the rest of the papers, walked out of the room and returned with a wheelchair. "Now, let's get you out of here."

Linc walked beside the wheelchair and Adeline reached over and tugged on his hand. When he bent down, she whispered, "Where have you been? You were gone a long time… I was afraid something happened."

"I'm sorry I worried you." He squeezed her hand and smiled. "I didn't like the idea of driving around without a spare, so I went to a local garage and purchased a new tire."

"You should have taken my credit card since it was for my vehicle."

"Nope. I'm the one who damaged the other tire. It's only right that I replace it." He straightened and turned to the nurse, who was pushing the wheelchair. "I'll go on ahead and pull our vehicle up to the door."

A few minutes later, Adeline was settled into the back seat of her Jeep with her foot elevated and Linc behind the wheel. "Are the boys and my mom okay?"

"They're fine. Ryan was at the airport picking up your mom when I called to let him know we captured Red."

"So, they didn't go to the safe house?"

"Nope. Lucy and Zane stayed at Ryan's house with Hadley, Sophia, the boys and Gunther. And Ryan and your mom went back to the boys' house to oversee the installation of the replacement windows and the cleanup."

"How did Ryan get replacement windows so quickly?"

"We did some work for the owner of one of the biggest building supply stores in Denver a few years ago. He was grateful for our help and said if we ever needed anything to call him. So, Ryan did." He pulled out of the parking lot and headed south.

"That's nice. Don't forget to have him send me the bill. Wait." She twisted to look out the back window. "This isn't the way to the lake house."

"I know. We need to get you back to Denver, so you can rest."

"But—"

"You're in no shape to be at the lake house hunting for the hidden documents. We need to get your prescription filled and get you settled at home. Don't forget you have an appointment with the orthopedic doctor tomorrow morning, which, by the way, I plan to drive you to since your mom will need to stay with the twins."

"What if something happens to the documents before we get to them? The police will need them to make a case against Red."

"Red is facing kidnapping and attempted murder charges. He won't walk free just because we haven't found the documents." Linc caught her eye in the rearview mirror. "There is no reason to believe Red is working with anyone. The bedtime story only mentioned one pirate. Copper...aka Red. Besides, the lake house is surrounded by crime scene tape and the sheriff has promised to have his men drive by throughout the night and monitor things. I'm taking you home. Ryan and I will head back up here and do a thorough search as soon as we can."

She wanted to argue with him, to tell him he needed her to help search. That he didn't know what he was looking for. But the truth was, she didn't have a clue what the treasure box looked like either. With a sigh, she leaned back and tried to get comfortable, regretting her insistence that they make the trip in her Jeep and not Linc's SUV, which would have had a roomier back seat.

"Do you want me to stop and buy a couple of pillows so you can get comfortable?"

His thoughtfulness touched her. So much about him reminded her of Dylan. All the characteristics that had drawn her to Dylan. How had she missed the similarities until now? Because she'd be so intent on doing her job without making close connections with the people she worked with. Now what? Adeline had built a bond with Linc. There would be no going back. Maybe a move to Florida would be best.

"Addie? Are you okay?" Linc asked.

His words jolted Adeline from her thoughts, and she shook her head. Big mistake. Adeline massaged her temple. "Yeah. Sorry. I zoned out a bit. The pain meds are making me groggy. I appreciate the offer, but I'd rather not waste any time by stopping."

"Are you sure? What about food? Do you want me to go through a drive-thru?"

"I'm fine, but if you're hungry, please get something for you. Although, I'm sure my mom is probably already cooking. A home-cooked meal is her answer to every illness, heartache or broken bone. And I'm positive she'll expect you to stick around and eat with us."

"Okay. No stops until we get you home. You just try to rest. I'll wake you when we get there."

"I never sleep in a vehicle. But don't worry about me. I'll just sit back here quietly."

He turned the radio on and selected an oldies station, lowering the volume so it was more background noise than anything.

Adeline took her jacket off and tucked it behind her neck. The doctor had said six weeks minimum in the cast. Guilt washed over her. She'd felt bad asking for a couple of weeks off after Vanessa and Isaac died. She'd now be out of work three times as long. The thought of looking for a job in Florida flitted through her mind again. Now that she'd decided she would raise the boys, she had to be pragmatic. Being a single parent was hard. There would be times she wouldn't be able to pick the boys up from school or attend their soccer games. She would need a support system in place. People who could fill in, in a pinch. Her mother and father.

Maybe the distance would help her regain perspective and her heart would realize she and Linc weren't meant to be. The fear that had gripped her when she'd thought Red would kill him had brought to the surface all the pain she'd experienced when Dylan had been murdered. She'd promised herself she'd never let her heart get involved and overrule her head again. But she had. The only thing to do was to put two thousand miles between them. If she made the move soon, maybe it would be like ripping an adhesive bandage off and her heart would heal quickly.

Her eyes drifted closed. She jerked them open and blinked repeatedly, fighting to stay awake. But the heaviness of her eyelids and gravity worked against her. She was so sleepy. Most likely the combination of the meds and the fact that she had been awake for thirty hours straight. Maybe she'd just close her eyes for a little while…

"Addie…" a voice called to her from deep inside a tunnel, but she couldn't respond. "Addie… You're home…"

She struggled to open her eyes but the curtain of fog was too thick. Fear washed over her. Where were the twins? She had to get to them. Keep them safe. Strong arms grasped her. She needed to fight back. Her entire body felt like jelly. The person lifted her and pulled her close. The rhythmic sound of a heartbeat penetrated her subconscious and a feeling of warmth and safety washed over her. She was home.

SIXTEEN

Lincoln slid behind the wheel of his SUV, started the engine and glanced at the clock on the dash. It was 10:17 a.m. The orthopedic specialist's office had been efficient. Adeline's appointment had been at eight thirty. They had gotten her straight back into the exam room, and she'd walked out on crutches an hour and a half later wearing a light blue cast that went from her toes to upper calf.

He turned to Addie, who had insisted on sitting in the front seat. "Are you sure you wouldn't be more comfortable stretched out in the back seat?"

"Only if you're going to wear a chauffeur's hat." She laughed. "I'm fine here. I promise."

"Okay, but let's adjust the seat so you have more leg room." He leaned across her and located the power button to move the base of the seat back. Pressing it, he looked up into her beautiful dark eyes and his breath caught. His eyes shifted to her full lips and back to her eyes. The desire to kiss her overwhelmed him. It was too soon. He didn't even know if she was open to the possibility of dating.

Linc jumped back and hit his head on the roof of the SUV. "Sorry." He rubbed the crown of his head. "I'm sure you can adjust your own seat," he mumbled, feeling more and more like a teenager with his first crush than the co-owner of a multimillion-dollar security firm.

"Are you okay?" she asked softly.

"Yeah. Bruised my pride more than anything." He settled into his seat and fastened his seat belt. "Are you good? Ready to go?"

She adjusted her seat, reclining it slightly, then nodded. "Ready. Eager to get back to the boys and my mom. I know Red's in custody, but I'm antsy about them being alone."

"You guys have been through a lot. It's only natural that you don't like them being out of your sight. But, like you said, Red is in custody, and he won't be getting out anytime soon." He squeezed her hand then shifted the vehicle into gear and backed out of the parking space. "I spoke with the sheriff in Grand County this morning. Red claims that he and Isaac were business partners until Isaac turned on him and took something that was his. He was trying to get his property back and hadn't intended any harm."

She scoffed. "Yeah, that's why he kidnapped us at gunpoint."

"He won't be dodging those charges. Thanks to the security system Ryan installed, we have it all on video footage."

"Did he say what he and Isaac had been involved in?"

"No. He won't give up that information. No one would incriminate themselves when the DA didn't have evidence of a crime."

She sighed out a breath and sank back in her seat with a groan.

"Are you okay? Do you have your medicine with you?"

"No. I don't plan to take any more of those pain meds. I lost almost twelve hours yesterday after taking the ones at the hospital." He felt her gaze on him. "Imagine my shock when I woke up on the couch in the living room just after midnight and didn't even remember how I got there."

His cheeks warmed as he remembered the way she'd fit in his arms. She had been the epitome of Sleeping Beauty. All he'd wanted was to keep her close where he could protect her now and for always.

Where had that thought come from? He shoved his wandering thoughts to the far recesses of his mind. There would be time to deal with the emotions he was feeling later, when he could sit down with Adeline and they could discuss things. For now, he needed to keep his focus on her recovery and finding the missing documents.

"I offered to take you upstairs, so you'd be more comfortable, but your mom said it would be easier to keep you downstairs, until you had crutches." He tapped the steering wheel. "Have you given any more thought to where the documents are hidden?"

"It's the only thing I can think about. I really thought Isaac hid them somewhere at the lake house."

"Ryan and I searched every inch of the lake house property last night. We didn't find anything. And the boathouse is a total loss. If the documents were in there, we'll never recover them."

"Thank you for searching. I can't believe you went right back to Lake Granby. You must be exhausted."

"Nah. Ryan drove while I napped, and we were back home by eleven, so I got around six hours of sleep last night." He activated his blinker and turned onto her street. "The only place we haven't checked that's connected to the lake house is Isaac's boat. Do you think the documents could be hidden somewhere on it?"

"I think it's probable. I'll look through the files in Isaac's office and see if I can find out where the boat is. Once I locate it, I'll contact the storage facility and find out when I can gain access to the boat."

I'll look. I'll contact. I can gain. What happened to *we*? After he arrived this morning, Addie had even tried to assert that her mom could drive her to the orthopedic appointment. Mrs. Scott, whom he had learned was a former schoolteacher, had insisted that she needed to stay home with the boys and help them get caught up on their missing assignments so they could return to school on Monday. Then Addie's mom had topped off her argument by insisting, since Linc had gone out of his way to do such a kind deed, it would be rude to decline his offer of a ride.

He couldn't help but wonder if Addie's sudden desire to stress her independent side had anything to do with the look that crossed her face the morning when they'd rowed ashore at Harry's house and she'd told Linc not to get himself killed. Linc still wanted to know what had caused that kind of pain to cloud her eyes, but now wasn't the time to ask about it.

A dull pain throbbed behind Adeline's right eye. She leaned her forehead against the passenger's-side window, the cool glass offering a moment's respite.

"I cleared my schedule for the day so I can stick around and help. A quick internet search should tell us all the marinas in the area," Linc said. "Then we can start calling to find out if they have Isaac's boat."

"There's no need for you to do that. Mom's here. She can watch the boys while I make calls. I'm sure you have other things you need to…" Her voice trailed off. A green

SUV was parked in the driveway. She hadn't been expecting company.

Linc activated the blinker and turned into the driveway. "Whose vehicle is that?"

"I don't recognize it." She scrunched her brow. "Could be a friend of Mom's who heard she was in town and dropped by to see her."

Linc pulled to a stop, put the vehicle in Park, hopped out and jogged around the front to her side. "Do people often stop by unannounced?" He snagged the crutches out of the back seat and held them out to her.

"I wouldn't say often, but it isn't unheard of. At least, not since Vanessa and Isaac passed away. Friends of theirs feel obligated to drop by and check on me and the boys, usually with a casserole or something." She tucked the crutches under her arms and slogged her way along the sidewalk. "I guess we'll find out who the visitor is once we're inside."

Now why had she said *we*? This would have been the perfect opportunity to send him on his way. Wasn't that what she wanted? For him to go about his normal life now that Red had been captured? Sure it was. But it would hurt the boys if he didn't at least tell them goodbye. They had been excited to see him this morning, bombarding him with questions about her injury and going on and on about how strong Linc was for carrying her indoors the night before. She'd feigned annoyance that they thought her weight would have been a burden for him, and everyone had laughed. It had been the perfect start to the day, even with a broken ankle and the looming orthopedic appointment.

The front door opened as they neared the porch, and

her mom stepped outside. "Good, you're home. You have a visitor in the dining room. A female officer from the navy. Here to ask questions about that man who attacked you." She waited for Adeline to make her way up the steps. "I just served your guest coffee, and I left the carafe and extra mugs on the buffet. If you don't need me, I thought I'd run to the grocery store."

"Thanks, Mom. You don't have any information to share about Red, so no need for you to hang around." Adeline paused for a moment to catch her breath. An avid runner, it surprised her walking with crutches was such a strenuous workout. "What about the boys? Are they going with you or staying here?"

"They're upstairs finishing their math assignment, so I thought I'd slip out without telling them."

Adeline laughed. "That's probably a good idea. Knowing you, if they went, you'd buy them all kinds of junk food."

A sheepish smile crossed her mom's face. "Of course, I would. They're my precious grandbabies. I can't say no to them."

"Funny. You never had trouble saying no to me when I was a child." She smiled and kissed her mother's cheek. "Thank you for being here. If you want to buy the boys a treat, that's fine. Just don't forget to pick up some healthy snack options, too."

"Deal. Now, if you both will excuse me, I'm going to grab my purse and get out of here."

Her mom disappeared into the back of the house and Adeline turned to Linc. "Ready to meet our guest?"

He frowned. "Yes, but I'm wondering why someone from the navy is here. We mentioned nothing to the sheriff about a possible navy connection."

"True. But if Red is still on active duty, or even if he's retired and receives a pension, the navy would be interested in the details surrounding his arrest and may have sent someone to help connect the dots."

"Okay, but we may want to keep the idea of hidden documents to ourselves. At least until we locate them."

"Agreed."

A thoughtful expression crossed his face, and he held out his hand to indicate that she should go first. Adeline hobbled down the hall and crossed the threshold into the dining room.

A woman several years Adeline's senior, dressed in a blue navy uniform, stood as they entered the room. "Ms. Scott, I'm Captain Penelope Warner. I appreciate you taking time to meet with me."

"Captain Warner. Please, be seated." Adeline glanced over her shoulder. "This is my boss Lincoln Jameson."

"What can we do for you, Captain Warner?" Leave it to Linc to get straight to the point.

"I'm here to ask a few questions about Robert Owens. I understand he's been arrested for kidnapping and attempted murder. Can you tell me more about the incident?"

Adeline exchanged a look with Linc then turned back to the older woman, who looked pressed and put together in her crisp uniform, her auburn hair in a low bun. Not a single strand out of place. Addie tucked her hair behind her ear and smoothed a hand over her wrinkled T-shirt, then plastered a smile on her face. "If you don't mind, I'd like to see your credentials before we answer questions."

A smirk briefly marred the other woman's features

before she shuttered her expression. "Of course." Captain Warner handed over her identification. "Satisfied?"

Adeline held the card so Linc could examine it, too, then returned it to Captain Warner. "Yes. Thank you."

"I'm sure you understand our need to be cautious." Linc turned to Adeline. "I think, before we answer questions, we should move to the living room where you can sit with your leg propped up. Didn't you say the doctor wanted you to keep it elevated to reduce swelling?"

"I'll be fine. I'm sure this won't take long. Will it?"

Captain Warner smiled. "Not at all. But I agree with Mr. Jameson. There's no point in you being uncomfortable." She scooted the seat she'd vacated back under the table and picked up the small satchel draped across the chair back.

Adeline wasn't used to being coddled and would have preferred answering the questions in the dining room and sending Captain Warner on her way sooner rather than later. She opened her mouth to argue but the concerned look on Linc's face stopped her. Instead, she turned and led the way to the living room.

Soon they were all settled. Adeline sat on the sofa, her leg propped up on an ottoman, and Captain Warner perched in the armchair to the left of her, facing the doorway.

"Now." Warner extracted a small notebook and pen from her bag. "Why would Lieutenant Owens want to harm you? What is your connection to him?"

"We're as in the dark about that as you are." Linc sat on the arm of the sofa closest to Captain Warner. "My employee called me Tuesday night when an intruder breaking into the house awakened her. He was gone by the time I got here, but over the course of the next thirty-six hours, he continued to make multiple attempts on Adeline's and the twins' lives."

"Captain Warner." Adeline leaned forward and fastened her gaze on the other woman. "Do you have any idea why Lieutenant Owens broke into my sister's house a week after she and her husband died? What was he looking for?"

"I assure you, the navy would also like to know what he was after. When I received the call of his arrest last night, I did a little digging and discovered Lieutenant Owens and your brother-in-law were stationed at NAS Oceana, in Virginia Beach. It's a large base, and Isaac wasn't a member of the SEALs, so there's really no way to know where or how they crossed paths. If they did so while there." Captain Warner closed the notebook then dropped it, along with the pen, into her bag. Standing, she crossed to the fireplace. "If I'm not mistaken, the setting of this painting looks like the Virginia Beach fishing pier."

"It is." Addie smiled. "The painting was a first anniversary gift from Isaac to Vanessa. He hired a local artist to paint it based on a photo someone snapped the day he proposed."

Linc had noticed the painting last night, when he'd settled Addie on the couch, but had regarded it as a piece of decoration and hadn't given it much thought. He examined the artwork. In the painting, Vanessa stood just off center in a white sundress, her long blonde hair blowing in the wind, with Isaac, in khakis and a white dress shirt, down on one knee holding out a ring box. The Virginia

Beach fishing pier stood in the background framed by a spectacular sunset.

The pirate hid the evidence he'd gathered against Copper in a treasure chest near his favorite body of water. The wooden frame of the painting was thick enough to hide any number of documents. Linc met Addie's gaze. Had she had the same thought?

He stood. "I'm sorry we weren't able to give you more information, Captain Warner. If you'll leave your card, we'll—" A frown crossed Addie's face. He'd done it again. Taking charge and saying *we*. "I mean Adeline will call you if *she* thinks of anything of importance."

A smile replaced the frown and his heart soared. With time and patience, he could learn to take a step back and not try to be in charge all the time. But they really needed to get rid of Captain Warner so they could look at the back of the painting.

"But I haven't finished," Warner protested as he handed her the bag she'd left on the floor beside the armchair. "I want to look—"

"I'm telling you the answer is sixteen. You got it wrong." Josiah's voice carried from the hallway.

"Let's ask Aunt Addie. I'm sure she'll know—" Matthew froze in the doorway, and Josiah plowed into the back of him.

"What'd you stop for?" Josiah stepped around Matthew, Gunther at his heels. "Oh. Sorry. We didn't know someone was here."

Gunther sat at Matthew's feet and growled. Matthew stood rooted to the floor with his eyes transfixed on Captain Warner. The tiny hairs on the back of Linc's neck stood at attention.

"Do you need help with your math?" Adeline swung her foot to the ground and grasped her crutches.

Josiah shook his head. "No. I know how to do it. We just came down for snacks." He raised his hands to display cookies and a blue drink in a flip-top bottle. "We'll go back upstairs. Come on, Matthew."

"Matthew? Are you okay?" Linc felt the sudden urge to race to his vehicle for the weapon locked in his glove box.

"You said Copper Penny was in jail."

Warner's face contorted into pure rage, and she pulled a handgun out of her bag. "I always hated that nickname."

Chaos ensued. Matthew screamed and dove into Adeline's lap. Gunther leaped to his feet and growled, baring his teeth in a defensive move. Josiah backed up a step. And Linc moved to position himself between the gun and the family he loved with all his heart.

"Freeze!" Warner demanded, her gun pointing at Linc.

Linc held up both hands, palms out, and shifted ever so slightly so his body blocked Adeline and Matthew. His mind reeled. Copper Penny was a woman. How had he and Adeline missed that detail?

Dear Lord, please let me stop her before she hurts Adeline or the boys.

SEVENTEEN

Never taking her eyes off the scene in front of her, Adeline kept Josiah in her peripheral vision. He clung to the side of the wall closest to the front door at the opening of the living room, his drink bottle pressed to his chest. Frustration and helplessness bubbled up inside her. She inhaled deeply and desperately tried to release her fears as she exhaled. She would not let her current situation prevent her from protecting her nephews.

"You don't want to do this." Linc spoke in soft tones. "I don't know what has led you to believe harming innocent people is the solution, but it isn't."

"Shut up! Let me think." Warner took one step to the right and glared at her. "Where's your mother? Get her in here. Now!"

"I can't. She went to the grocery store as soon as we arrived home. She won't be back for at least an hour." *Please, Lord, don't let Mom come back too soon.*

Gunther started barking and crouched low, as if he were going to attack Warner. Adeline's heart raced. If the German shepherd leaped at Warner, the woman might discharge her weapon and hit one of the boys. She could not allow that to happen. "Gunther, here, boy." She tapped the side of the couch and he bound over to her. "Heel."

He sat on his hind legs, and she rubbed the fur between his ears. "Good boy."

Tears soaked Adeline's shirt as silent sobs racked Matthew's body. She wrapped her arms around him and pulled him tight. "Shh. It's okay. I've got you," she murmured in his ear.

"Okay, everyone on the couch." Warner waved the gun, indicating Linc and Josiah should sit.

Linc took two steps backward and bumped into the coffee table he'd pushed aside earlier to make room for the ottoman. Adeline pried Matthew's arms from around her neck and settled him on the sofa beside her then reached forward to move the ottoman.

"Easy. Any sudden moves and the gun might go off. And I can't be responsible if it hits one of the innocents you're worried about protecting." Warner smirked.

Fear reached its icy fingers into her chest and tried to suffocate her, but Adeline refused to allow fear to take over. She wrapped her heart in the knowledge that God was in control and He loved them. "I was clearing the walkway. As you can see, the ottoman is big and heavy and is not on casters. There is no way I can make a *sudden* move with it."

Adeline moved the ottoman so it no longer blocked her, though she still wondered what help she'd be in this situation.

"I can move the coffee table," Matthew said quietly, and he got off the couch and moved the wooden table out of Linc's path.

"Now, sit," Warner commanded.

Matthew scampered to his spot, right up against Adeline. Linc backed up until his calves bumped against the sofa then sat on the edge like a caged tiger waiting for an opportunity to pounce.

"Okay, now you." Warner looked at Josiah and jerked her head. "Get on the couch."

His gaze glued to the woman with the gun, Josiah stood on his tiptoes and shifted left. Half of his little body disappeared behind the wall that separated the living room from the entryway. What was he doing? The panic button on the alarm system. Pressing it would send a silent alarm to Protective Instincts' security team. Ryan had showed the boys the new security system after he had installed it, and had taught them how to use it. Smart boy. The hope that swelled inside her was short-lived.

Warner marched toward Josiah and grabbed at him with her free hand. He laughed, ducked under her outstretched arm and ran into the room. Adeline bound to her feet and a blinding red-hot pain shot up her leg. She yelped, grabbed her leg and fell backward onto the couch. Linc leaped forward and placed his body between Josiah and Warner.

Adeline searched for something within reach that she could use as a weapon, but to no avail.

"Sit. Down. Now," Warner commanded Linc, the gun once again pointed at his chest.

Linc hugged Josiah to his side and walked them both backward.

"Not. Him." Warner locked eyes with Linc and smiled. "Just you."

"That's not happening. Josiah stays with me."

"Josiah, is it? Well, Josiah, do you want to see me splatter—"

"No!"

"He's eight years old," Adeline and Linc said in unison.

The auburn-haired woman cackled. "Even so. You get my drift, don't you, Lincoln? I will not warn you again. Follow my directions or that is exactly what these boys will witness."

Adeline reached out and tugged on Linc's hand. They needed to stall for time, but they couldn't afford to antagonize the woman with the gun. He looked at her and nodded. Then he sat down, his hand resting on Josiah's shoulder.

"Josiah, it seems like your mommy and daddy forgot to teach you any manners. Children should respect their elders and follow instructions." She shifted the gun to where it pointed at Adeline. "Now, if you don't want to see anyone get hurt, I need you to do as I say. Do you understand, Josiah?"

Josiah flipped open the top on his juice bottle and took a drink. Then he lifted his face to Captain Warner. "Yeah, sure."

Adeline had never heard her nephew sound so flippant toward an adult before. Obviously, he didn't know the *don't antagonize the person with the gun* rule. Linc murmured something to Josiah under his breath. Josiah shrugged Linc's hand off his shoulder and shifted slightly to the left.

"Okay, so, Josiah. Do you know what a zip-tie is?"

"Of course, I do. I'm not a baby." Again, with the attitude.

"Josiah. That's enough," Adeline reprimanded her ward. She understood her nephew was nervous and scared, but provoking Warner would not help anyone in the long run.

"Oh, it's okay, *Auntie Addie*." Warner laughed. "I think

Josiah and I understand each other." She motioned to her bag sitting on the floor, where she'd dropped it in front of the fireplace. "I want you to get the zip-ties out of my bag and give them to your aunt. She will tie your brother's hands and feet so you can see how it's done. Then you will zip-tie your aunt and Mr. Jameson."

Josiah crossed the room, sat down cross-legged on the floor and placed his drink bottle beside him. Then he dug into the bag and pulled out a handful of plastic ties.

Warner backed up a few steps and looked over her shoulder at Josiah. "Do you understand what you need to do?"

"Yeah. I sure do." He grabbed his juice bottle, jumped to his feet, pointed the bottle at Warner and squeezed. A stream of blue liquid hit the captain square in the eyes. She threw up her hands, trying to block the onslaught, and Gunther charged, knocking her to the ground. The gun flew out of her hands and, when she tried to get up, the German shepherd growled, baring his teeth, and pinned her to the floor.

Josiah raced to the couch and flew into Addie's arms.

Linc grabbed a zip-tie and quickly fastened Captain Warner's hands together. Then he hauled her to her feet and escorted her to the armchair, where he fastened her feet together, too.

Josiah turned and looked at Warner. "See, I understood the assignment. Disarm the threat. My daddy taught me that."

The woman who'd spent the last thirty minutes terrorizing them sat stone-faced, damp hair plastered to her head and bluish-purple juice stains on her white shirt collar.

Gunther sauntered over to the couch, and the boys

dropped to the floor and hugged him. "Good boy, Gunther," Josiah praised the German shepherd.

"You were great, too, Josiah." Matthew hung his head. "I guess I failed as the big brother."

Josiah slung his arm around Matthew's shoulder. "No, you didn't. You're the one who taught me how to be brave."

"Matthew." Adeline ruffled her nephew's hair. She was hesitant to break up the boys' tender moment but needed to satisfy her curiosity. "How did you know Captain Warner was Copper Penny?"

"Dad let me look through his photo albums when I hung out in his office. Sometimes he'd tell me stories about his sailor friends that were in the pictures." Matthew narrowed his eyes and glared at the woman tied in the chair. "One time I asked who she was and Dad said she was nobody. A bad Penny who turned up every once in a while. When I saw her earlier, I thought of what Dad said, and I knew she was Copper Penny."

The twins looked at each other, bound to their feet and gave Adeline a tight hug. Her heart swelled. She wrapped her arms around them, returning their embrace. "I'm proud of both of you."

The sound of a siren in the distance caught Adeline's attention. "Okay, guys. Time to take Gunther out of here. Get him a treat then put him in the backyard. Make sure the gate is closed and latched. Then get your snack and hang out in the kitchen for a while. Okay?"

"Yes, ma'am," they said in unison and led Gunther out of the room, casting furtive glances at the woman who had waved a gun at them earlier.

Adeline was sure she'd have to answer a lot of questions later. She prayed she would find the right words to help them feel safe and that they wouldn't suffer long-term trauma from the event.

"I wouldn't think this was over just yet, if I were you," Warner said. "Believe me, I've talked my way out of tighter spots than this. Before I'm finished, I'll have anyone and everyone believing you attacked me, and that I was only defending myself. It will be a piece of cake, especially since you don't have any evidence to support a motive for me attacking all of you."

"Ah, but you're mistaken. We have evidence. Or should I say, Isaac had evidence. And thanks to you, I know where it's been hidden this entire time." Adeline turned to Linc. "Would you mind taking down the painting for me?"

"I'm happy to do it." He crossed to the fireplace, took the painting off the wall and turned it around to reveal a long, slender, metal box fastened to the inside of the frame.

Linc pried the box loose and carried it to Adeline. "I believe you have the key."

She slipped off the necklace and inserted the key into the lock. Willing her racing heart to calm, she turned the key and lifted the lid. Inside there were documents, a USB drive and a handwritten note from Isaac.

Vanessa, please forgive me. I never meant for the mistakes of my past to hurt you and our boys. Your love helped me become a better man. I had hoped to keep my past sins buried, but when I realized Penelope was putting the country's future in jeopardy, I couldn't sit back and do nothing. She had to be stopped, and I was the only one who could do it, even if it meant I'd spend the rest of my life in jail. However, if you're reading this, I can only guess things didn't go as planned and I'm no longer with you. You need to get these documents to the NCIS immediately. And, my darling wife, please make sure my boys know that while I was not perfect, I loved you, them and my country with all my heart. Thank you for loving me. Forever yours, Isaac.

Tears flowed down Adeline's cheeks, and she scrubbed them away with the backs of her hands. The sound of the sirens grew louder, and Linc patted her shoulder. "I'll let them in."

She nodded and turned to Penelope Warner. "It looks like Isaac was thorough in his documentation. I'm sure this is enough to put you away for the rest of your life, but I will also put in a formal request with the police to have the investigation into the accident that took Vanessa's and Isaac's lives reopened. You will pay for killing them."

Ryan and Linc entered the room with two police officers close behind. Linc briefed the officers on the events that had transpired.

Ryan crossed to the couch and knelt beside Adeline. "Are you and the boys okay?"

"Yes." She released a ragged breath. "Physically, anyway. May take a while to heal emotionally."

"I understand. It took Hadley, Sophia and I some time to heal after Sophia's abduction. We found a Christian counselor to help us work through all the emotions. I'll send you his contact information." Ryan patted her hand. "In the meantime, I'll go keep the boys company while the officers interview you and Linc."

"Thanks." Her voice cracked.

Ryan enveloped her in a warm, brotherly hug. "Hang in there. You're doing good. Vanessa and Isaac couldn't have left the boys in better hands than yours. Trust that. And trust God to show you the way as you navigate this new path in life."

Adeline nodded, unable to get words past the lump in her throat. She had failed at keeping evil away from the boys, and she didn't know if any amount of counseling would help them get over the trauma of having a gun pointed at them. But Ryan was right. Vanessa and Isaac had trusted her to raise their sons. She would make mistakes along the way. But with God's guidance and the help of family and friends, she would figure it out.

Linc dropped a twenty-eight-pound bag of dog food into the back of his SUV, alongside Adeline's and the boys' suitcases, and closed the gate. Mrs. Scott had driven the boys and Gunther to Adeline's condo hours earlier, after the child welfare caseworker the police had called in to assess the situation had given the okay. Although Linc knew the officers and the caseworker had only been doing their jobs, the threat of the boys being taken away from Addie had added an extra layer of doom to an already stressful situation. Fortunately, the caseworker had come to the same realization as everyone else. The boys were where they belonged. Their aunt loved them and would go to the ends of the earth to protect them.

The caseworker had suggested counseling for the boys to deal with the grief of losing their parents and the trauma of the last few days, and Ryan had called Hadley for the contact information of the counselor they'd used. The caseworker was familiar with the counselor and said he would have been the one she recommended. She'd do a follow-up visit with the boys before she closed the file on them, but as long as they were having weekly sessions with the counselor, the follow-up would be a formality.

Linc took his phone out to check the time and saw a text from Ryan, requesting that he call when he had a moment.

His best friend answered on the first ring. "Hey, buddy. Are you still with Adeline?"

"Yes. We're about finished up here. I'm getting ready to drive her home."

"Good. I hope she and the boys are able to get some rest. You, too."

"Thanks. But I'm sure you didn't ask me to call to tell me that."

"No. I spoke with my contact at NCIS. Are you ready for this? Penelope and Robert are siblings. My contact said it will take months to determine what secrets they sold and to whom, but Isaac's documents are thorough. So that will give them a good starting point in the investigation. However…" Ryan sighed.

"However…?" Linc's chest tightened. Could this family handle more bad news?

"My contact said, even though he's deceased, it would be impossible to keep Isaac's name out of the investigation or the news. And, depending on the outcome of the investigation, Isaac's estate will be liable for any fines levied against him."

"I'll let Addie know. Hopefully, she can keep the boys from hearing most of what the news will report about their father. As for the rest, she missed an appointment with

Isaac's attorney the day Matthew was almost abducted. I'll advise her to contact him as soon as possible."

Disconnecting the call, Linc stifled a yawn and scrubbed his hand across his stubbled cheek. He needed food, a hot shower and a shave, and not necessarily in that order. His needs would have to wait until he drove Adeline home and ensured she, the boys and her mom were settled.

He turned then jogged up the walkway. Time to lock up the house and help Addie to his vehicle.

"I saw that," Addie said, standing in the shadows of the porch steps.

He stopped at the bottom of the steps and laughed. "What did you see?"

"The yawn. I knew you had to be exhausted. You should have gone home long ago. I could have called a rideshare service to drive me home."

He walked up the steps and reached her side. Then he cupped her face with his hand. "Do you really think I would be happier at home not knowing if you were still here dealing with things or if you had made it safely to your house?"

"You've gone above and beyond the past few days, and I don't know what I would have done without you. You've been a true friend."

Lincoln dropped his hand. *A true friend.* Her words stung as if he'd been burned by fire. Didn't she feel the connection between them? It went beyond friendship. She had to know that.

She cleared her throat, swung the crutches around and made her way over to the cushioned bench. Leaning the crutches against the side of the house, she dropped onto the bench and patted the seat beside her. "We need to talk."

His heart dropped. *We need to talk* weren't words any man wanted to hear. Fine. He picked up the throw pillow that occupied the other side of the bench and tossed it onto the nearby chair. Settling into the spot he'd just cleared, he turned to face the woman who'd stolen his heart. The light streaming through the living room windows illuminated her beautiful face.

He had hoped to postpone any kind of talk about their relationship and where it might lead for a couple of weeks, so she'd have time to adjust to her new life with the boys, but if this conversation took the turn he thought it might, he would have no choice but to lay his feelings on the line. Of course, if she didn't feel the same, it didn't matter how much he hated the *friend* label, he'd accept it and do whatever he had to, to bury his feelings. After all, he'd resigned himself to bachelorhood long ago. He could do it again.

Dear Lord, being relegated to the sidelines of her life will be painful. I selfishly want more, but as long as she and the boys are still a part of my life, it will be okay.

"You and Ryan were so gracious to grant me a couple of weeks' leave after Vanessa and Isaac died, and I hate to leave Protective Instincts in a bind." She waved her hand at her cast.

Relief washed over him. She was worried about her job, not their relationship.

"Normally, I'd work—"

He caught her hand. "Don't worry about it. We have plenty of people to cover while you're recovering. I'll even—"

"No." She tugged her hand free. "I'm telling you we're moving to Florida. The boys need more stability, and I need help. I have to move closer to family. If it wasn't for my injury, I'd work out a notice. As it is, my cast will come off the week before school is out." Adeline shrugged, a frown on her face. "I can't work a notice after that. The boys will need the summer to settle in to a new routine before they start at a new school…"

Frustration bubbled up inside him. He had not been expecting this.

Help me, Lord! Give me the right words. I know I said I could accept just being friends, but I can't imagine not seeing her every day.

He shoved his hand through his hair and exhaled. "You don't have to do this. You have help right here in Denver. We'll schedule your jobs around the boys' schedules. And I'll cover whenever you need someone. I'm sure Ryan and Hadley would be happy to help, too."

"I can't ask you all to do that."

"You're not asking. Haven't we already proven we'll be here for you?"

She touched his cheek. "Yes. And I love you—all— for it. But I can't ask you to commit the next ten years to helping me raise the boys."

"You do, don't you? Love *me*, that is." He captured her hand and pulled it to his lips. "I saw something in your eyes at Lake Granby when you told me not to get shot."

Tears shimmered in her eyes, and she bit her lip.

The idea of causing her the slightest bit of emotional pain shook him to his core, but if he didn't tell her his true feelings, he'd regret it forever, even if she still walked away. "I think someone hurt you and you're afraid to put your heart on the line again. I get it. When I was in the military, I had friends killed in combat. Many of them left behind wives and children. I would attend funerals and offer my condolences to the families, and I'd see the devastation and fear in the faces of the ones still alive. That's when I decided if I was going to continue in this line of work, I'd never have a wife or children of my own."

A lone tear slid down her cheek, and he brushed it away with his thumb. "But I was wrong. You and the twins have taught me that while losing someone you love leaves an unfathomable void, never having loved at all is an empty existance."

"You're right. On all accounts. Dylan was a detective with the Dallas PD. We dated and I really cared about him. He was shot and killed during a hostage situation. He shouldn't have died that night, and I miss him. But my life *is* better for having known him." She smiled.

"You said I was right *on all accounts.*" *Please, say it. Tell me you feel about me the way I feel about you.*

"Yes. But… My feelings for you don't change anything. The boys need stability that I can't give them here. They need family."

"They have family right here. Me, Ryan, Hadley and Sophia. But most of all, you. And, if you're happy, they will be, too."

Adeline opened her mouth to speak, but he placed a finger on her lips. "I just need to say one more thing. Please. Then I'll listen to whatever it is you want to say."

She nodded, and he dropped his hand.

"It took me too many years to find you. I don't want to lose you now. I want to date you and see where these feelings take us. If you stay and decide it's not what's best for you and the boys, we'll all move to Florida. You, me, the twins and Gunther. Because wherever you are is where I want to be."

"You would do that for me?"

"No, I would do that for *us*."

Adeline placed her hands on his cheeks, her eyes shining. "The boys and I will stay in Denver. We'll make it work. I never dreamed I could have it all, but with you by my side, I'm beginning to think I can. I love you."

"And I love you." He lowered his head and claimed her lips.

Thank you, Lord, for answered prayers.

EPILOGUE

Adeline pulled into the driveway of the home she'd purchased over the summer, after deciding she and the boys needed a fresh start in a home without bad memories surrounding it. Since her condo had been too small for her, two growing boys and a German shepherd, the only option had been to purchase a new home. Fortunately, she'd been able to find the perfect house in a gated community. And, as an added bonus, Linc lived in the same neighborhood, only three streets away.

She put her Jeep into Park, glanced at the clock on the display panel and cut the engine. It was almost six o'clock. Two hours later than she'd planned on arriving home. Although the twins had probably had so much fun with Linc they hadn't even noticed she was late, she hated to take advantage of his generosity. In the past seven months, he had far exceeded the role of boyfriend. A smile lifted the corners of her mouth and her heart fluttered. Even after all these months, her heart swelled every time she thought about the strong, loving relationship she and Linc were building.

Linc and the twins had gotten close, too. He took them fishing and camping, and picked them up from school at least twice a week. She appreciated his willingness to jump in and offer a helping hand whenever she needed one, but she needed to talk to him and Ryan about cutting back on her hours, especially during the school year. Fourth grade was a lot harder than third grade, and the boys had a lot of homework each evening. And they were growing up way too fast. She needed to be present for them and enjoy the time she had with them while they were still young. One day, they'd find their independence and not need her as much. But that day wasn't today.

She hummed as she made her way to the front porch. A piece of white paper taped to the door fluttered in the wind. Her name was written on the paper in bold black letters, in Matthew's best penmanship. A note? She reached out and pulled it free.

> *Aunt Addie, take a deep breath and let go of the stress of the day. Then enter through the door and follow the trail to the treasure that awaits you.*

She opened the door and stepped inside the entryway. Matthew and Josiah, dressed in matching dark suits, white button-down shirts and black ties, greeted her.

"Welcome." Matthew bowed.

"What's going on?" she asked.

"You'll find out soon enough." Josiah smiled, turned, and offered her his elbow. "May I escort you?"

Matthew rushed to stand on the other side of her and mimicked Josiah's stance. "He means, may *we* escort you?"

Joyous laughter bubbled up inside her. "Yes, you *both* may." Adeline placed her hands through the crooks of their arms.

They led her past the living room, to the den and out

onto the deck. Her breath caught. The backyard had been transformed. White twinkle lights lined the stone walkway all the way to the gazebo, which was also decorated with lights.

"We gotta go get Gunther." Josiah hugged Addie then headed indoors.

"We'll be back." Matthew smiled, gave her a hug and trailed his brother into the house.

She followed the lighted path to the gazebo Linc and Ryan, with the help of the twins, had built as a housewarming gift. It was her sanctuary. The place where she spent quiet time in prayer each day as she drank her morning coffee and watched the sunrise. Adeline had planned to hang the lights herself, but it looked like her guys had done it for her as a surprise. They were, all three of them, such a blessing.

Adeline froze at the base of the steps. Linc stood in the center of the gazebo, in a black suit and tie, and his arms full of yellow roses. This was more than a thoughtful gift from him and her nephews. Releasing a slow breath, she tried to calm the butterflies that danced in her stomach to the high-tempo beat of her heart.

Holding out his hand, Linc descended the steps. She placed her hand in his and allowed him to guide her into the center of the gazebo, decorated on the inside with flowers and greenery and a scattering of rose petals on the floor.

"What…?" She looked around then settled her gaze on his handsome face. "What is all this?"

"You don't know?" He smiled and settled the bouquet of roses in her arms. "In those old romantic movies that you enjoy so much, this is the ending. But in reality, it's only the beginning."

Happy tears pooled in her eyes, and she wiped at them with the back of her hand.

"I wasn't looking for love. Or a ready-made family. The moment I stepped into your sister's house the night of the break-in and found you barricaded in a room with your two nephews, I had an overwhelming urge to protect—all three of you—like I've never felt before. And protecting people is what I do, every day, for a living. But this was different." He captured her hand, caressing the back of it with his thumb. "For the first time, you—my no-nonsense employee who was and forever will be one of the toughest female bodyguards I have ever employed—showed a vulnerability that hit me like a sucker punch in the gut. I knew, no matter what, I would not leave your side until you and the boys were safe."

The tears she'd tried to hold back freely streamed down her face. She laughed. "Now you're making me ugly cry."

"Impossible. There's nothing ugly about you. From the inside out, you are the most beautiful, selfless woman I've ever known." He stuck his hand into his pocket, pulled out a ring box and opened the lid to reveal a beautiful emerald-cut ruby solitaire with two small diamonds, one on each side of the center stone.

She gasped. It was the most beautiful ring she'd ever seen.

"This was my grandmother Jameson's engagement ring. She gave it to me right before she passed away fifteen years ago. And she told me when I found a Proverbs 31 woman, to put it on her finger and make her my wife. *For her price is far above rubies. The heart of her hus-*

band doth safely trust in her..." He dropped to one knee. "Adeline Scott, I love you with all my heart. If you'll have me, I promise to stay by your side for always. To be there in the good times and the bad as your protector and biggest supporter. Will you marry me?"

Gunther barked. She looked around and saw the twins standing near the bottom of the gazebo, with Gunther sitting between them. Gathered behind them were her parents, Linc's parents, Mrs. McCall, and Ryan, Hadley and Sophia.

"Don't forget to say yes, Aunt Addie!" Josiah yelled, and the small crowd laughed.

She turned back to Lincoln. "Yes! Most definitely, yes!"

He stood and placed the ring on her finger. A perfect fit. Just like the man, and the life they were building as a family of four. Linc claimed her lips in a kiss as the gathering cheered.

* * * * *

If you liked this story from Rhonda Starnes,
check out her previous
Love Inspired Suspense books:

Rocky Mountain Revenge
Perilous Wilderness Escape
Tracked Through the Mountains
Abducted at Christmas

Available now from Love Inspired Suspense!

Find more great reads at www.LoveInspired.com.

Dear Reader,

Sometimes in life we find ourselves on paths that are vastly different from the ones we planned to travel. Such was the case for Adeline. No matter how much she tried to resist accepting the responsibility, she soon discovered being the twins' guardian was the right path for her. There was no other job she wanted more than to love and protect her nephews, especially with Lincoln by her side.

I don't know about you, but like Adeline, I have taken detours down paths I thought weren't for me, only to discover I was exactly where I was meant to be. With God's guidance and loving people by our side, even the most difficult path can be more easily traversed.

I would love to hear from you. Please connect with me at www.rhondastarnes.com or follow me on Facebook @AuthorRhondaStarnes.

All my best,
Rhonda Starnes